I0638691

Sugar Boss

Sugar Daddies #2

Charity Parkerson

Punk & Sissy Publications

—·—

COPYRIGHT

—Warning: This book is intended for readers over the age of 18. Some of my books contain allusions to past abuse and trauma.

Editor: Vicky Reese

Photographer: EricBattershell

Cover Model: Eric Ten Brink

CONTENTS

AUTHOR NOTE

SUGAR FIGHTER AND SUGAR BOSS have concurrent timelines. When the story reaches present day, you'll see where the timelines collide. On a different note, Zander has a very dark past. While his past is never shown, only alluded to, if you're extra sensitive to violence you might be bothered. I'm a firm believer in happy endings. Zander deserves his more than most.

—·—

INTRODUCTION

ZANDER DIDN'T GET WHERE he is by playing nice. Everyone has a price. Maverick is no exception.

Maverick knew when he met Zander he'd have to set boundaries. Zander Kapra already has more than any one man should, and Maverick doesn't intend to join the list of faceless men Zander has probably bedded. It doesn't help that Zander is in the position to make or break Maverick's MMA career. Maverick would never let any man have that kind of power over him.

As owner of all the Luna hotels and casinos on the West Coast, Zander controls who can enter bet fights in his cages. Maverick caught his eye months ago. Every Friday night, Zander makes a point of being wherever Maverick is, stalking him. Waiting for his chance. There's something about the cocky fighter. Zander has to have him, but Maverick doesn't treat him like everyone else. It doesn't matter. Zander didn't get where he is by playing nice. He gets who he wants. Whenever he wants them. He won't allow Maverick to be an exception.

From day one, Maverick and Zander struggle for dominance, but Maverick has bigger problems than Zander's overbearing ways. Zander's secrets might be a harder punch than he can take.

CHAPTER 1

HIS STARE WAS DISTRACTING as hell. Every Friday night. Same seat. Same light-blue gaze. Maverick knew exactly where his sexy stalker was at all times. He no longer fought to win. Maverick fought because those goddamn beautiful eyes watched his every move. So much blood stained the mat inside the cage, Maverick couldn't begin to guess what color it had originally been. Cage fights weren't for the squeamish. All Maverick cared about was the adrenaline pumping through his veins and the roar of the crowd assaulting his ears. He had no illusions. They weren't cheering for him. It was all about the money. Their addiction to gambling. None of it was for him. It took everything he had not to look the sexy blue-eyed man's way. Maybe one person was there for him.

Tonight, his match lasted longer than usual. His muscles screamed, but his arms lifted in victory. There were no speeches here. One fight ended. Another pair squared off. Maverick ducked from the cage. An ice-blue gaze met his. Dark suit. Perfect, long blond hair. Beautiful. They'd never met, but Maverick knew him. Everyone knew Zander Kapra. As Maverick passed him, their gazes never wavered. Maverick's heart sped. Heat grew between them. Damn. The dude was amazing, but—like every Friday night—it was over as quickly as it began. They never spoke.

Maverick didn't understand how a complete stranger could consume him, but this man did. Every Friday night, Maverick went home alone with the fantasy of him. Maybe tonight, he'd find someone new. Someone real. Fingers encircled his arm, stopping him before he made it inside the locker room. He spun. A behemoth of a man stared him down at him. His dark eyes didn't look mean exactly. It was more like he had never met anyone or anything that scared him. Maverick was pretty sure that included bears. The dude was massive.

"Mr. Kapra would like to know if you'd join him for dinner?"

His thick accent was a surprise. It caught Maverick's attention. His gaze shifted over the man's shoulder, landing on the light blue eyes that always set Maverick's skin on fire. The heat staring back at him almost burned him alive. Maverick's mouth watered. Damn, he'd never been more tempted. He focused on what was obviously a bodyguard. "Tell Mr. Kapra, if he works up the courage to ask me himself, I'll say yes." The way the guy's dark eyebrows lifted in surprise might've been funny if Maverick had stayed around to enjoy it. Instead, he dipped inside the locker room before the guard or messenger or whatever he was thought of a way to respond.

It wasn't until he had hot water streaming down his body that Maverick realized he was smiling like an idiot. He tried rearranging his features. Possibly he'd made a mistake, but Maverick didn't think so. Men like Kapra probably always got their way. Maverick was interested, but if Mr. Kapra didn't want him badly enough to tax himself even a little, there was no sense in Maverick wasting his time. He'd find out next Friday if he'd completely fucked up any chance of meeting his delicious obsession if his new friend didn't come to his fight. A wave of sadness washed over Maverick. What if his sexy blue-eyed admirer didn't show? He couldn't imagine not seeing him in his usual front row seat.

With his shower out of the way, keys and gym bag in hand, Maverick headed for the door. He tried not to think about the possibility of never seeing the man again. As he stepped out into the crowded hallway, he found his path blocked. Blue eyes held him hostage. Expensive cologne had him breathing deep.

"So, you doubt my courage?"

He had a smooth voice. One Maverick wanted to listen to all night. Maverick wanted to play with him. "Not if you're here to ask me to dinner."

His mouth twitched, as if he found Maverick humorous. He held out his hand for Maverick to shake. "I'm Zander."

"Maverick," Maverick said, shaking Zander's hand. He didn't want to let go. It was over too soon. Up close, Zander was even more gorgeous than Maverick thought. There were laugh lines around his eyes. Delectable.

"I know," Zander said, forcing Maverick to pay attention to their conversation. "Would you like to have dinner with me?"

Maverick's gaze slid to the two men who stood nearby, eyeing the crowd in case they had to take someone down to protect their boss.

"Will we be eating alone?"

"We'll be alone at a table."

Maverick met Zander's stare. "Where would you like to meet?"

Zander's mouth twitched again. It was obvious he didn't know what to make of Maverick. "Are you afraid to ride with me?"

Maverick didn't back down. "My mama always told me not to accept rides from strangers."

As Maverick's southern accent deepened, Zander's obvious amusement kicked up a notch. His eyes swam with laughter. "We could head upstairs and visit the hotel restaurant. That way you're in no danger of being molested or turning up dead in a ditch."

Maverick dipped his chin and motioned toward a nearby elevator while trying not to laugh at Zander's statement. After all, he'd started it. "The upstairs restaurant sounds good to me." When Zander turned away, Maverick's gaze dropped to his ass. Damn, he was perfect. He was a few inches shorter than Maverick, but at six-five, everyone was. Zander was slender and screamed money. Maverick had always had a weakness for beautiful, expensive men. As they rode the elevator to the main floor, Maverick couldn't stop staring. There was some gray mixed in Zander's light-colored hair. Maverick had to take a breath to get his racing heart under control. Age meant experience and stamina. Damn. Zander punched all the right buttons. As the door slid open, Zander's gaze moved Maverick's way. For a moment, they held each other's stare. Neither of them smiled. There was too much heat between them. This man didn't play games. Maverick felt it in his gut. It took all Maverick's concentration to keep his breathing steady. Every time he'd seen Zander, he'd known it was only a matter of time before they ended up here.

At his appearance, staff raced to accommodate Zander, finding them a private table in record time. Maverick stashed his bag under the table. Zander's guards didn't sit with them, but they stood close enough that Maverick never forgot they were there.

"How does a boy from Texas end up here?" Zander asked, focusing his full and powerful attention on Maverick.

Maverick didn't bother asking how he knew where Maverick was from. Zander Kapra probably knew everything about everyone and was only asking to make conversation. "By way of the Marines," Maverick said, letting Zander have his way. "I was stationed here and quickly learned I wasn't made for military life, but I was born for this place. The moment I could get out, I did. I trained to become a firefighter and stayed."

Wine and food appeared at the table even though they'd never ordered. Maverick wanted to chafe against being given a meal he might not want, but it was steak, and he fucking loved steak. He couldn't bitch.

Zander eyed him as if testing his reaction.

Maverick knew when to pick his battles. He cut into his food.

Zander waited until Maverick's mouth was full to respond. "I meant, how does a boy from Texas end up here," he said, tapping the table. "Fighting in a casino and not on the circuit. I've seen several of your matches. You have talent. If you wanted, you could be famous. For some reason, you've chosen not to try."

Maverick carefully swallowed and took a sip of his wine to give himself time to think before answering. Plus, he wasn't entirely certain how to take Zander's observations. In the end, the truth was always the best. "Talent isn't enough to be an attention grabber. There are countless men who can do what I do and want to be famous. You have to be a showman or special in some way to make it to the top. I'm not. Special, that is," he added, since Zander's expression hadn't changed.

"Do you know who I am?"

Maverick didn't see any point in lying. "Yes." He imagined everyone who fought professionally knew Zander Kapra. He owned a chain of hotel casinos where most West Coast fights were held and heavily bet upon—Luna Hotels. The hotel they currently sat in.

Zander cocked his head. His face remained blank. "Did you accept my dinner invitation because of who I am?"

A smile tugged at Maverick's lips. He couldn't help it. He had accepted for that reason, but not in the way Zander meant. It wasn't the hotels or money. Nor did it matter what Zander could do for his career. For Maverick, it was the countless Friday nights with Zander's stare eating him alive. It was the unquenched lust that owned Maverick every time their eyes met. "No."

"Then why?"

"Because you asked," Maverick answered without hesitation.

A small smile touched Zander's lips, making him look more like he had an evil secret than he was amused. "No matter your reasons," Zander said, waving off Maverick's answer. "I could do more for your career than you've ever dreamed. If you're interested."

Maverick's smile fell. "I'm not."

Zander's eyebrows rose. "Why?"

Maverick tossed back his wine before he lost his chance. It looked more and more like their time together was coming to an end. He flashed Zander a smile he didn't feel. "I love every-thing about MMA. This is my fami-ly. I'd be lying if I said I didn't want a title or for everyone to know my name. The thing is, I'm not an id-iot. If someone offers you everything you want, but they're also in the po-sition to take away everything you love—run. The moment they think they no longer own you or you stop dancing to their invisible strings, they will destroy you, and nothing is ever free. So, I guess the real question is—why did you ask me to dinner?"

Zander's mouth lifted in one cor-ner in one the sexiest smirks Maver-ick had ever seen. His gaze wouldn't waver from their delicious fullness.

"You know why," Zander said forcing Maverick's gaze back to his. "My strings aren't invisible. You should stay with me tonight."

A bright smile, one that was out of his control, snapped to Maverick's lips. "You should ask me out again. When you're not trying to buy me, that is."

"Is that your way of telling me no?" Zander didn't look annoyed. The opposite, in fact.

Maverick couldn't stop teasing him. "I'm not that easy. You should get to know me. Unless you're only looking to scratch an itch, then you should go away. I'm not your guy."

Zander didn't bite. He stood. "Let me walk you to your car."

Maverick didn't budge. "With your security escorting us?"

"Of course," Zander said, holding out his hand for Maverick. "They're used to seeing everything while seeing nothing." An unexpected sexy-sounding chuckle escaped Zander, making Maverick's breath catch. "Unless you plan to molest me inside your car. If so, I'll find them something else to do."

With a shake of his head, Maverick grabbed his bag and stood. "You're safe in my company," he said as he accepted Zander's outstretched hand.

Their fingers linked. Maverick spent a moment wondering if his knees would hold him at the pressure of Zander's palm against his. He had never been so instantly enthralled with anyone.

Heads turned their way as they passed. Pride rose in his chest. Maverick knew he was out of his league. Most likely, he'd never hear from Zander again, especially since he'd made it clear he wasn't for sale, but—for the moment—this gorgeous man was his.

"You're smiling," Zander said without looking his way.

Maverick tried rearranging his features.

Zander turned his head. Blue eyes focused on him. "Don't stop. Happiness looks damn sexy on you. I meant for you to tell me your thoughts."

With that one statement Zander made it more than obvious he was used to people anticipating his needs before him. "You didn't ask for them."

A loud sigh escaped Zander. He looked away. The sound had Maverick's smile reappearing. "Thank you for having dinner with me. I would very much like to know why you're smiling."

Maverick didn't answer until they were at his truck. He opened the driver's side door, found a pen and an old receipt, and jotted his number on the back. Maverick held it out to Zander. "I'm smiling because I think you'll call."

Zander's fingers closed around the paper and Maverick's hand. He tugged, pulling Maverick against him. Maverick automatically dipped his head the second their bodies touched. Their lips met. The world disappeared. If Zander's security stood inches away or had abandoned them at the door, Maverick couldn't say. He lost track of everything except the man kissing him. It wasn't explosive. Instead, it was sexy as fuck. Zander held Maverick's bottom lip between his, sucking lightly while making no attempt to deepen their kiss or touch him in any other way. Maverick's usual controlling nature disappeared. Zander owned him in that moment.

Zander took a step back. Maverick's body leaned forward as if chasing after Zander with no input from Maverick's brain. "Good night, Maverick." Zander turned away before Maverick found his voice to respond.

"Goddamn," Maverick whispered under his breath as he watched Zander go. He had a feeling he'd met his match.

Pytor stood beside the back door of a black BMW 7, waiting for Zander. Yaro was already behind the wheel. He didn't need to give his men instructions. Both men had been with Zander for years. They already knew he obsessed over things to the point of being considered psychotic. They couldn't judge nor would they. As he crossed the underground parking lot, Pytor opened the door. Once Zander was safely ensconced in the back seat, the large Russian with odd eyes circled the car and joined him. Yaro waited for his opening before following Maverick at a distance. Just as they did every Friday night. Zander wouldn't sleep unless he knew his fighter made it home safely.

As they pulled into the parking lot of the townhomes where Maverick lived, Zander eyed Maverick's red Dodge Ram parked in its usual spot. Yaro slowed, allowing Zander time to see Maverick's living room light flare to life. He nodded, satisfied Maverick would be fine. Yaro pulled away, and Zander settled in for the drive home. His mind wandered. He could still remember the first time he'd set eyes on Maverick Abney. Zander hadn't paid much attention to Maverick's match. He'd been there on business. But the moment Maverick stepped from the cage, sweat coating his skin, Zander's gaze had followed him. The way Maverick's shoulders and hips moved—like a predator. He'd mesmerized Zander. The following Friday night, Zander had made a point of visiting the next hotel where Maverick had been scheduled to fight. As Maverick left the cage, their gazes had locked. For a moment, there was no air. Maverick's eyes were the most beautiful shade Zander had ever seen. They were the color of honey with dark lashes making them seem lighter. Beautiful.

Zander was a patient man. He never rushed into anything. Considering his position, he couldn't openly trust anyone. He'd studied Maverick. Followed him. There was nothing about Maverick's life Zander didn't know. For someone so gorgeous, Maverick lived an oddly solitary life. He worked, went to the gym, and fought. There weren't many nights with friends or dates. Maverick seemed to be on auto-pilot—existing but not really living. Just like Zander. It wasn't for lack of time. Zander was a busy man, but he'd make time for the right people. Nothing wowed him any longer. Maverick was too young to already feel that way. There was a fire inside Zander every time he looked at his sexy fighter. He craved showing Maverick everything. A smile pulled at Zander's lips. He should've known Maverick would be the type who wouldn't want anything Zander had to offer. Zander couldn't lie to himself. He was intrigued. The sexy confidence that rolled from Maverick's tongue with every word had Zander burning to control him.

He dug Maverick's number out and programmed it into his phone. Zander would call, but not tonight. Tonight, he wanted Maverick to simmer. Maverick needed to spend some time considering all the possibilities of what being with Zander could do for him. Zander fully intended to take over Maverick's life. Maverick needed to think about that.

CHAPTER 2

IT WAS DAYS LIKE today that doubled Maverick's desire to fight professionally, making enough money to quit his day job. Coming off a twenty-four-hour shift was hell. His clothes stank. He was exhausted, and the sun was coming up. Despite it being seven in the morning, all Maverick wanted was a beer. Well, a shower too. A groan escaped him as he eased down on the couch and kicked his feet up on the coffee table. He was so fucking tired, there wasn't a word to describe it. His phone rang, pulling a growl from deep in his soul. He dug out the device ready to rip into whoever hated him so much they'd call the second he got home. An unfamiliar number stared at him from the screen. His brows pulled together in confusion as he answered. "Hello?"

"I called."

At the sound of Zander's smooth yet bossy tone, Maverick's dark mood and exhaustion fell away. He bit back a chuckle. "So, you did."

"Does that mean you'll see me tonight?"

"Hmmm," Maverick said, pretending to think it over. "I suppose I have to. Since you called that is." And he'd started worrying about mid-shift that he'd never hear from the gorgeous hotelier again. A low rumble of laughter caressed Maverick's ear. His eyes fell closed at the sound. Everything about Zander was beyond sexy.

"Am I to be trusted to pick you up this time?"

Maverick didn't answer right away. He liked the idea of having a way to leave. After all, he didn't know Zander. Not really. With Zander's money and power, he already had the upper hand. All Maverick had was the power to say no.

"I take your silence as your answer. How about I give you an address and you show up around eight?"

"Sounds good," Maverick said, trying not to let his relief show. He needed time to sleep. Before he knew it would happen, his voice took on a seductive edge. "I like being in control."

That damn sexy laugh came through the line once more, challenging Maverick's ability to breathe properly. "I'm not opposed to handing over the reins for one night. As long as I get to see you again."

"Why now?" Maverick asked before he could stop himself. "After six months of watching me," he clarified, in case Zander didn't understand his question.

"Because I was free this past weekend," Zander answered. There wasn't an ounce of hesitation in his voice. Maverick liked how Zander was always straightforward. Zander didn't stop. "It's unusual for me to have an entire weekend without a single meeting scheduled. I'd hoped to have some time alone with you. You turned me down. Now, I have cleared more time for you."

Maverick's cheeks hurt from smiling. He got the feeling Zander didn't get told no often. He needed to learn the world didn't run on his schedule. "To be fair, I didn't completely turn you down. I said you should get to know me. You never know, once you do, you might not want anything to do with me."

"It's odd," Zander said, sounding puzzled. "It's almost like you want me to admit I want to fuck you and nothing more, but that's not true. If it were, I would've already had you. Are you always this difficult?"

Maverick bit his lip, trying to hide his smile despite Zander not being able to see him. Zander was so fucking self-assured. It was almost overwhelming. Luckily, Maverick loved confident men. He dropped his feet to the floor and leaned forward, setting his elbows on his knees. "When you're straddling my lap, you can tell me if I was worth it. Text me the address. I'll be there." Maverick hung up without giving Zander time to respond. He stared at his phone, waiting. Zander didn't disappoint.

Zander: *400 Ocean Port. 8 p.m.*

Maverick: *I'll be there.*

For a full ten minutes, Maverick stared into space while holding his phone. Since that kiss, Zander had ruled his every thought. The sexy bastard had already been in his head before Zander had blown his mind, but now. Fuck. He couldn't stop thinking about those lips. He wasn't sure how long he could resist Zander. Maverick leaned back, dropped his head against the back of the couch, and closed his eyes. They were essentially strangers. No doubt, they had nothing in common. Once Maverick gave in, and they fucked, he'd probably never hear from the sexy billionaire again. An odd ache spread through his chest at the thought. Maverick hadn't been this interested in anyone in a damn long time. Life had been gray for a while. Mundane. He wasn't ready to go back to feeling like there was nothing to look forward to.

Maverick tuned out the depression that tried storming its way in. For as long as he could remember, he had suffered from unexplained black moods. Right now, all he wanted in his head was Zander. Damn. Zander's confidence was hot as hell. Maverick had never met anyone like him. He could only imagine what Zander was like in bed. Was he controlling, or did he like to be dominated after being in charge all day? A smile pulled at Maverick's lips. It was a little insane how badly Maverick wanted to bend Zander to his will. Maverick had always been a controlling person. His need to dominate had led him down many paths. That's why he fought—for release. It was also one of the reasons he was single. Maverick was too intense for most people. Zander could take it. Maverick felt it in his bones.

His body stirred. Maverick took a deep breath. His palm collided with his erection through his jeans. He stroked. Those blue eyes were in his head, making him desperate. He needed sleep. Otherwise, he wouldn't be worth a damn when he saw Zander tonight. His cock jerked. A groan rose in Maverick's throat. He needed release, or he might fall on Zander like a crazed animal later. Maverick was tired of jacking off. He'd been single way too long, and uninterested in everyone he met. Without thought, he unbuttoned his jeans. His erection grew as if seeking his hand. Maverick swallowed. An image of Zander on his knees fired to life in his head. Maverick's heart sped. He could practically feel Zander's hot mouth sucking him off already. Maverick slid his zipper down. His phone buzzed, killing the fantasy. With a sigh, he checked the face.

Zeke: *Are you up for a spar session?*

Maverick glanced down at his hard dick. Zeke was a title holder. Sparring with him always challenged Maverick. Maybe that's what he needed—sore muscles and an empty mind.

Maverick: *Yep. Give me fifteen.*

After pushing from the couch, Maverick made it five steps before his phone buzzed again. He didn't bother checking it until he made it to the bedroom and found his workout gear. When he opened his messages, a smile appeared at the first sight of Zander's name.

Zander: *Get some sleep.*

It was like Zander watched him and knew Maverick didn't intend to go to bed like he should. Maverick chewed his bottom lip and pondered his next move. In the end, he couldn't resist texting Zander back.

Maverick: *Don't worry. I'll be rested enough for whatever you have in store for me.*

He didn't look away from his phone. Maverick didn't want to miss the moment Zander responded. Zander didn't make him wait long.

Zander: *I'm not worried about that. You've had a long night. Get to bed.*

Maverick: *Soon.*

With a shake of his head, Maverick tossed his phone aside. Part of him wanted to chafe against being told what to do. Another part of him reveled in Zander's concern. Worry meant he wanted more from Maverick than sex. Right? Maverick drove himself crazy with that question. It wasn't until he was halfway to the gym that another question hit. How had Zander known he'd had a long night?

The doorbell chimed, echoing throughout the house. Zander was already on his way to the door before Maverick ever touched the bell. Security had alerted him the moment Maverick breached the property. When the door swung open and Zander set eyes on Maverick, Zander's mind went blank. Maverick's hair was swept back away from his face. Still, a strand fell across his eyes as the door opened. Zander feared himself in that moment. Maverick should be scared. There was no low Zander wouldn't sink to in order to have anything he wanted. Considering how badly he craved Maverick, there was zero excuse for Maverick not running for his life.

"I think I barely escaped a cavity search to get through your security," Maverick said, skipping the hellos.

Zander kept his tone as bland as Maverick's. "You didn't escape that. I told them I would search you later."

Even Maverick's eyes smiled as his lips curled at the corners. "This place is amazing."

Since Maverick's gaze never wavered from Zander's face, Zander had no clue how he'd know. Zander stepped aside, letting him inside. "Sorry for the crazy security. Next time, they'll recognize you and it'll be easier."

"You're so confident there'll be a next time." Maverick's voice was a low purr as he passed Zander, forcing Zander to take a deep breath to control his need to hasten this game.

Zander closed the door. "Would you like a tour?" Before the question completely left his lips, Zander found his back shoved against his closed front door. Maverick's large frame pinned him against the cool wood. While holding Zander's jaw in a tight grip, Maverick covered Zander's mouth with his. Zander's heart slammed against the wall of his chest. He could barely breathe beneath the onslaught of Maverick's attack. Maverick's tongue slid along Zander's bottom lip. Zander didn't hesitate to let him in. Holy shit. Maverick's kiss was so much better than he ever imagined. Zander hadn't pushed with their last kiss. This was... damn. He never wanted it to stop. It was over as quickly as it started.

Maverick pushed away. "I'll take that tour now."

Zander wasn't having it. This boy liked to start shit. After snagging Maverick's t-shirt, he towed Maverick back in, and took control. With Maverick's bottom lip held between his teeth, Zander massaged Maverick's erection through his jeans. Once the roar of satisfaction passed over Maverick being turned on, Zander allowed himself a moment to be impressed by how thick Maverick was. He shoved Maverick away and stepped around him. "Would you like to start downstairs or upstairs?"

"I'm at your mercy."

Yes. He was. Maverick just didn't realize how true those words were yet. Instead of responding, Zander led Maverick through the house, showing him the top floor first. "I don't come up here very often, to be honest," Zander said as they cleared the top step. Maverick was so close, Zander could feel the heat radiating from his skin. He'd never been more aware of anyone in his life. "Half the rooms are empty." A soft chuckle escaped Zander at the admission. "I bought the house for its location. Not its size." He flipped on a set of lights that lit up the third-floor balcony, overlooking the ocean. He led Maverick outside. "You probably won't believe me, but I would've been just as happy with a one-room shack as long as I had this view."

The wind ruffled Maverick's hair as he stared out at the ocean. Zander fought the urge to touch him. Maverick didn't look like a man who needed anyone. It was a thought that had Zander willing to go to any length to make Maverick dependent on him. Maverick's sexy lips turned up in the corners as his gaze swung Zander's way. "I'm not saying I don't believe you, since this is an amazing view, but I can't see you in a one-room shack. Have you even been in a one-room anything?"

Zander's hair flew in his face when he turned his head. He pushed it behind his ear. "You'd be surprised."

Maverick's smile slipped away. His expression turned serious. "I'd love to hear the story."

"Maybe if you keep coming around, I'll tell it."

With a shake of his head, Maverick leaned his elbow on the balcony railing and eyed Zander. "You're not making it easy for me to get to know you."

The remark hit home. Zander switched his gaze to the crashing waves and braced his hands against the railing next to Maverick. Chances were better than not that Maverick wouldn't like Zander much once he learned anything about him. The thing was—Zander wasn't playing with Maverick. He wanted Maverick to know him. The real him. He let some of his Russian accent peek through, tossing away years of careful practice. "Growing up, we had nothing. I spent many days standing in food lines, praying we would not starve."

Maverick's heat pressed closer. "How did you end up here? With all this?"

Zander turned his head and held Maverick's gorgeous gaze. "By using my fists. The same way you will."

A shy smile, one Zander had never seen before touched Maverick's lips. "I already told you, I'm not a showman. It's okay. There's nothing wrong with fighting in your casinos. Have you had dinner?" Maverick asked, obviously uncomfortable with the conversation turning his way.

Zander boxed Maverick in, bracing his palms on the railing on either side of Maverick's body. Since Maverick only had about three inches on Zander, he didn't have to tilt his chin far to hold Maverick's stare. He couldn't let Maverick get away. "You're exhausted. Did you not sleep as I suggested?"

"Ordered."

Zander shrugged. "Same thing. I see you didn't take my advice. Have you also not eaten?"

Maverick's mouth turned up in one corner, as if Zander's questions amused him. "How did you know I worked a twenty-four-hour shift?"

"Always assume I know everything. You'll be less likely to drive yourself crazy that way," Zander answered without answering.

"If you know everything, what do I want right now?"

An unexpected laugh rose in Zander's throat. He took a step back. "Alcohol. Come on. I'll fix you a drink."

"That is just fucking uncanny," Maverick grumbled, following on Zander's heels as he headed back downstairs.

Zander led Maverick inside his office while hiding his smirk. He motioned for Maverick to sit on the large leather sofa lining one wall while he headed for the bar in the corner. No matter how hard Zander tried, he couldn't stop inspecting Maverick's every reaction to each new thing. Maverick sank into the expensive leather. He stared down at the couch as if confused by the piece before poking it a few times.

"Holy crap. This must be the best couch I've ever seen. What kind of leather is this?"

Zander poured a few inches of vodka in a glass and downed it before answering. "I have no clue. All I did was tell a designer not to let me down and wrote them a check." He downed another glass, savoring the burn, before filling one for Maverick.

"Is this where you spend most your time?" Maverick asked Zander as he crossed the room.

"Unfortunately, no. I spend most of my time at one of the hotels, dealing with whatever bullshit is happening for the day."

"You don't sound happy. Whenever I ask you anything about your life," Maverick clarified, as if Zander didn't understand. Zander wished he hadn't felt Maverick's claim all the way to his bones.

"I'm happy right now." Zander couldn't have stopped the confession if he tried. He loved the way Maverick's gaze moved over his body, as if he would be his next meal. In fact, the way Maverick watched him had Zander setting their glasses aside. Maverick had said Zander could tell him if he was worthwhile once he was straddling his hips. Without a word, he set one knee on the couch, and then the other until he stared down at Maverick from his lap. Maverick didn't push him away. In fact, his arms encircled Zander, pulling him closer. His palms slid up Zander's back. At Maverick's urging, Zander pressed as close as he could get. His lips brushed the shell of Maverick's ear.

"I'm straddling your hips."

"Am I worthwhile?" Maverick asked before he kissed Zander's shoulder.

Chill bumps rose on Zander's skin. His dick stirred. Maverick made him hungry. "You have no idea." Zander was certain Maverick was a hundred of everyone else. There was no length

Zander wouldn't go to in order to win Maverick.

Maverick moved faster than anyone Zander had ever met. In a flash, he had Zander trapped beneath him on the couch. His mouth covered Zander's, cutting off all oxygen as he forced his way inside. Their tongues met. Maverick's touch gentled. He brushed Zander's jaw as he explored Zander's mouth. Zander had never been more blown away by anyone. Maverick was overbearing. His weight kept Zander pinned in place. Yet, Maverick's touch was soft, making Zander want to beg. He craved the hard fucking Maverick always promised with his stare. Zander wanted the kink he saw hidden behind Maverick's playful smiles.

"Stop holding back," Zander begged against Maverick's lips.

A low chuckle vibrated around their entwined tongues as Maverick deepened their kiss. Zander fought a growl. Maverick made him insane. Zander was an adult with no reason to play games. He liked what he liked and wanted what he wanted. No shame.

Maverick's teeth sank into Zander's bottom lip before scraping his chin and moving to Zander's neck. "You have no patience," he said against Zander's throat. His hand moved slowly down Zander's body. "All you have to do is relax. I'm not going anywhere."

Not going anywhere, including forward, was exactly what Zander feared. "I'm not surprised to find myself at your mercy."

Maverick didn't seem bothered by Zander's observation. He barely paused in sucking on Zander's neck to respond. "Why is that?"

"Why am I not surprised or why am I always at your mercy?"

Without hesitation, Maverick's hand snaked its way beneath Zander's shirt, stroking his stomach. "Why aren't you surprised?"

"Because you always win," Zander answered as he massaged every inch of Maverick he could reach.

Maverick went still. His sexy honey gaze found Zander's. "What?"

"I've been watching you for months." Zander didn't care if Maverick knew he was insane. He'd eventually find out anyhow. "You always win. It seems this is no different."

Maverick's expression turned amused. "I don't always win. In fact, life loves kicking me, especially when I'm down."

Zander stroked Maverick's arms, savoring their hard lines, and deep valleys. "I've never seen it."

"Stick around. You will," Maverick said, going back to nipping at Zander's throat.

Not if Zander had anything to do with it. He wouldn't let anything bad touch Maverick ever again.

Maverick pushed his shirt higher. Cool air brushed Zander's stomach. "Goddamn," Maverick breathed. "Your body is fucking amazing. What kind of fighting did you say you did again?"

Zander writhed beneath Maverick. "Street fights, but not for many years. Why are you still talking so sensibly?"

Without answering, Maverick slid lower. His tongue found Zander's abs. Before Zander had time do anything more than suck in a hiss, Maverick was back, nipping at Zander's bottom lip. "Fuck. I was turned on before I discovered what you're hiding beneath your clothes. Now, I don't even know what to think. You're too beautiful to get fucked on a couch."

The frustration was real. Zander was ready to scream. He'd never met a bigger tease in his life. Zander wasn't the type to ask for permission. He pushed until Maverick sat up, and then he dropped to his knees at Maverick's feet. "I choose where I play." Zander held Maverick's stare as he opened Maverick's jeans, setting his erection free. His mouth watered as the soft skin of Maverick's dick filled his palm. Maverick didn't fight. In fact, he looked more turned on than any man should. He stared down at Zander without blinking. Zander didn't disappoint. He stroked. Maverick's lips parted. A flush touched his cheeks. All thoughts of arguing seemed to disappear.

"I've seen the way you looked at me, leaving the cage these past months. You've wanted me just like this," Zander taunted. "On my knees." He licked Maverick's shaft while holding his stare. "Have you jacked off in the shower picturing me like this?" Zander massaged Maverick's cock, tormenting him with the perfect pace for quick results. "Or do you hide under the covers, stroking your dick and fucking your toys while chanting my name?"

Maverick's breathing turned labored. His hips lifted as he raced toward the orgasm Zander's fast pumping promised. Switching positions, Zander moved higher. He kept a steady pace, jacking Maverick's dick while teasing him with sucking kisses. Zander nibbled Maverick's earlobe and swiped the shell of Maverick's ear with his tongue. "You're so close. I can feel it. You love the way my palm feels, tugging at your hard dick. Would you prefer my tongue? Maybe you'd rather be inside my ass. Hot. Tight. Milking you when I come."

Maverick's muscles tensed. His body jerked. Zander clamped down on Maverick's cock, choking off his cum before a drop spilled, stealing his pleasure at the last moment. The pained cry that tore from Maverick's lips was like music to Zander's ears. Zander was jealous. When the time came, and he let Maverick come, his orgasm would be so hard it would drain him for the rest of the night. Zander hadn't felt that way in years.

He loved knowing he could make Maverick fly.

Zander shushed Maverick as he kissed a path down his body, going back onto his knees. He urged Maverick to lose his pants. Once he was bare from the waist down, Zander swiped his tongue across Maverick's crown before going back to pumping his cock, and tormenting Maverick with his words. "I want you to fuck my mouth like you want to tear up my ass, Maverick. This time, I'll let you come, as long as you don't hold back. Don't worry. I can take it. Show me how badly you want me."

Maverick's rage-filled gaze held Zander's as he buried his fingers in Zander's hair and yanked, forcing Zander's mouth to his dick. "That's it," Maverick praised as he pumped inside Zander's mouth, hitting the back of his throat with bruising force. "Suck harder, Zander. Swallow it."

Zander followed every command because he knew the truth. He might be the one on his knees, but he was the one in charge. In that moment, he owned Maverick. Maverick would do anything for Zander as long as Zander gave him release.

"Jesus, you're amazing," Maverick said, sounding desperate as he openly fucked Zander's throat. Maverick threw his head back, baring his teeth as he strained toward release. Zander shoved Maverick's knees wider and pushed two fingers inside Maverick's ass, fingering him as he sucked. Saliva ran down Maverick's erection and soaked his balls and asshole, easing his entry. Everything was soaked, including the couch beneath Maverick's ass. Zander curled his fingers inside Maverick, searching for the spot that would drive Maverick insane. He found it and massaged. A loud moan filled the room. Zander soaked through his underwear with pre-cum. His lust was crippling.

A cry tore from Maverick. Hot cum filled Zander's mouth. It rolled from his chin and choked him. He swallowed as fast as he could, but he'd let Maverick's cum build, forcing multiple orgasms from Maverick at once. Zander couldn't swallow the whole load. He let it flow, coating Maverick's lap.

In an unexpected move, Maverick's hand found Zander's throat. He squeezed, lifting Zander from the floor until he was sprawled across Maverick's chest. The mess between them soaked Zander's clothes as Maverick's tongue filled his mouth. He licked and sucked as if searching for every lingering drop of his cum on Zander's tongue. Zander had never been more turned on in his life. Maverick's teeth sank into Zander's bottom lip hard enough Zander tasted blood. His cock jerked and leaked inside his pants. He could barely breathe through the lust.

Maverick never released his hold on Zander's throat. The move wasn't choking, but Maverick let him know who was in control. Maverick held Zander away just enough to meet his stare. His eyes swam with dark lust. He was dangerous in that moment. "When I fuck you, it'll hurt, but you'll still beg me for more."

Zander swallowed down the whimper rising in his throat. He wanted that. Craved the pain.

"Get cleaned up," Maverick said, stroking Zander's face and neck while eyeing him like he might hurt him any second. "I'm taking you out."

CHAPTER 3

THE ROAR OF THE crowd around Zander seemed muted in the face of his desire to see Maverick. He barely stopped himself from sitting on the edge of his seat and searching the room for any sight of the sexy fighter like a teenager with his first crush. A bouquet of gorgeous pink roses appeared beneath Zander's nose. He automatically reached for them. "What's this?"

Pytor's large frame filled the seat beside him, taking up too much space. He shrugged. "I intercepted a delivery man trying to get them to you."

Zander eyed the roses. He didn't think he'd ever gotten flowers before. There was no card. "Did the delivery person say who they were from?"

Pytor flashed him an irritated look as if he thought Zander was an idiot. That's what he got for treating his guards like family. No respect. "Your giant fighter, of course."

Biting the inside of his cheek to hide his smile was automatic. If he'd learned nothing from being with Gio, he'd learned not to ever show happiness. Happiness was a weakness. Something to be exploited. Even though Gio had been dead for three years, some habits were hard to break. Zander hugged the bouquet a little tighter on the sly. He could tell Pytor and Yaro we're taking great pains not to look his way. They'd been with him for too long and knew him too well. He appreciated more than he could say for their discretion, letting him have his moment.

While Zander's attention was on the flowers, Maverick stepped inside the cage. Zander's gaze snapped to his sexy fighter. Compared to Zander's riches, Maverick had nothing. Yet, he'd bought Zander a gift. Not just any gift, but something useless that would be dead in days.

Maverick's head turned in Zander's direction as the rules were read. His mouth lifted in one corner in the world's sexiest smirk. He confused Zander. After the incident in Zander's office, Maverick had taken him to dinner, refusing to let Zander pay. Now, the flowers. It was almost as if Maverick was wooing him. Like he didn't realize he already had Zander.

Maverick always looked like he didn't care how the match ended. That's one of the ways the guy got in his opponent's head. Zander noticed it the first time he'd seen Maverick fight. Tonight, his "I don't give a fuck" stance seemed more exaggerated than usual. Rather than trying to psych out his opponent, Maverick kept flashing heated glances Zander's way. Zander's face hurt from trying not to smile. This boy... he drove Zander insane with an all-consuming need to call Maverick his.

Once the bell rang, it became twice as obvious Maverick wasn't really trying. He merely toyed with his opponent. Anyone paying attention could see Maverick pulling his punches and missing holds. The first weak hold placed on Maverick had him tapping out. Zander shook his head. He ran his tongue over his teeth, fighting his smile as Maverick passed.

This man—he was cocky as fucking hell. He'd thrown his match. Lost. On purpose. Zander wasn't stupid. It was a test. Maverick wanted to see if Zander would still chase him even if he wasn't winning.

He didn't let Maverick get far. Zander was on his feet before Maverick cleared the front ten rows. He closed the distance between them, skimming his fingers down Maverick's spine, reveling in his sweat soaked skin. Maverick glanced over his shoulder. His eyes flashed with heat the instant their gazes met.

"Come home with me."

Maverick turned and walked backward, obviously uncaring if he mowed people over. "You still want a loser?"

"I want you, even if you never win another match, but you're no loser. No matter how many fights you throw," Zander added with a laugh and unconsciously hugging the roses to his chest.

Maverick stopped moving. Zander didn't. Not until only inches separated them and the flowers halted his forward progress. Maverick dipped his head and spoke close to Zander's ear. His breath fanned across Zander's skin. "There's only one way you'll have me inside you tonight."

"Name your price," Zander said without hesitation. He'd pay any amount.

"You have to come home with me." Maverick held his gaze for a moment before walking away.

Zander shook his head. His smile was out of control. Maverick fought him at every turn. He waved Pytor close. Pytor leaned in for Zander's instructions. "Change of plans. I'll need you to keep a discreet distance."

"Of course, Mr. Kapra." With a nod to Yaro, they moved away. The pair would still keep him safe, but no one would know it. For two men who should stick out anywhere they went, the pair were damn good at staying out of sight. If Maverick needed to feel he was in control, Zander would let him play. Either way, Zander still won.

Zander was always quiet to the point of unnerving—like he'd gone to some damn finishing school that had taught him to be seen and not heard. Maverick loved Zander's voice. It was smooth and sexy and turned even hotter when his accent peeked out.

Even though they were parked out-side Maverick's apartment, Maverick made no move to leave his truck. "Do you like your flowers?"

Zander's gaze dropped to his lap, as if he'd forgotten he was holding them. He fingered one of the petals. "Yes, thank you."

Maverick plucked them from his lap and set them on the dashboard. "Let's leave them here, so you don't forget them in the morning."

For a moment, Zander eyed them with this bottom lip held between his teeth. He made Maverick wonder if he intended to snatch them back. Instead, his gorgeous blue gaze swung Maverick's way. "Won't they die out here?"

"They look pretty healthy. If they do, I'll buy you more." It was as if Zander had never been given flowers. They died. That's all flowers did, but Zander's gaze kept skirting their way, as if he was genuinely concerned about them. Maverick reached for Zander's hand and brought it to his lips, forcing Zander's attention his way. "I promise," he said, swiping a kiss across Zander's knuckles. "They'll be fine. You should worry over what I'm about to do you instead."

Zander's mouth lifted in the world's sexiest smirk. "You keep bragging, yet we're still sitting here."

"Hmm," Maverick hummed. He'd never met anyone who challenged him the way Zander did. Maverick wanted more. Instead of arguing, Maverick grabbed his gym bag, and leapt from the truck. Zander did too, stealing Maverick's chance to play the gentleman. Since Zander hadn't let him open the truck door, he stood still, waiting for Zander to come to him. He linked fingers with Zander and led him to the building.

Zander's presence was so powerful Maverick could feel the raw energy pulsing from him as he followed Maverick inside his apartment. He didn't bother turning on the lights. After tossing his gym bag aside, Maverick locked the door. Zander stood still, waiting. Silent. Nevertheless,

Maverick could feel his stare, even in the dark.

Maverick peeled off his shirt and tossed it toward his bag before linking his fingers through Zander's. He headed for the bedroom. He flipped on a small lamp near the bed, giving him just enough light so he wouldn't miss out on a single sexy inch of Zander's body. Still Zander didn't make a sound. Unlike the ride home, Zander's silence was oddly comforting—like they were stoic in the face of something powerful.

At the edge of the bed, Maverick sat and pulled Zander to stand between his knees. Zander's gorgeous gaze watched Maverick's every move.

While holding Zander's stare, Maverick slowly unbuttoned Zander's shirt. When the material hung open, Maverick pushed the shirt and jacket down Zander's arms, baring his upper body. Zander's body was amazing. Maverick couldn't get past how much beauty Zander hid beneath his clothes. He'd been hooked on this man before he'd caught a peek at Zander's body. Now, Maverick wanted to stroke every inch. He equally wanted to hear Zander's every thought. Maverick wanted to know why he stayed hidden behind a stern expression and expensive suits. It was obvious he worked damn hard on his body. There was so much about Zander that he kept to himself. Maverick craved all of him. Without thought, Maverick lightly brushed his fingertips down Zander's chest and stomach.

"You're being amazingly gentle for someone who warned me last night you'd hurt me." Zander's observation came out in barely a whisper, as if didn't want to break the spell Maverick wove with his soft touch.

An unexpected smile tugged at Maverick's lips. "Sometimes I'm more intense than I intend. Now that you're here, I can't imagine ever hurting you, even for the sake of pleasure."

While still holding Zander's gaze, he slid Zander's belt loose. He undid the button of his pants and slid down Zander's zipper. Zander never looked away, as if transfixed by Maverick's actions.

"I thought about you all day." Maverick focused on his hands, working Zander's clothes free, as he made the admission. If Zander found the confession ridiculous, Maverick couldn't see it in his eyes. Maverick knew he was getting attached too quickly. He couldn't stop. Zander probably had a different man every other night, making similar claims. For Maverick, Zander was unique. Maverick couldn't pinpoint exactly what it was about Zander, but he had Maverick's attention.

"You were stuck in my head today too."

At Zander's quietly spoken confession, Maverick met his stare. His breath caught. Zander was serious. Maverick came to his feet, forcing Zander to take a step back. While holding Zander's stare, Maverick pushed Zander's pants and underwear down his hips, letting gravity carry them to the floor.

"Forget what I said last night. I'd like to make love you, savoring each moment I'm inside you. Tell me how you like it and I'll make you love it."

Zander finally touched him. His hands slid across Maverick's hips, before finding their way to the button on Maverick's jeans. "I don't care as long as I can kiss you and see your eyes. Those are the two things about you I can't resist."

"I'll work on making that list longer," Maverick promised as he captured Zander's lips. Their bare chests met as their tongues entwined and Maverick went up in flames. He pushed and pulled, ensuring there wasn't a stitch of clothing standing between them before his hands found the perfect globes of Zander's ass and lifted. Their erections bumped as Maverick maneuvered Zander onto the bed beneath him. The second he settled between Zander's thighs, Maverick caught himself moving against him. He needed more of their cocks brushing. Zander kissed him like a man who'd been denied too long. Like Maverick's kisses were oxygen. Everything about Zander was perfect, as if he had been designed for Maverick. It wasn't outer beauty, even though Zander possessed that in spades, it was something deeper that tempted Maverick beyond all reason. He'd never been more scared of losing someone who wasn't his. Zander felt too good to be true. Maverick knew any second, he'd open his eyes and realize Zander never existed. The thought sent a shot of fear through Maverick, forcing him to tear his mouth away and stare down at Zander. Zander's lips were swollen from Maverick's rough kiss. His cheeks were flushed and his breaths labored. He stared back at Maverick, looking every bit as shell shocked as Maverick felt.

Maverick focused on the gorgeous blue eyes he couldn't get out of his head and rocked against Zander. He reached between them, palming their erections and stroking. The sensation of their dicks against each other in Maverick's hand was amazing. A sexy-sounding moan escaped Zander. Maverick wanted more. He slipped down Zander's body, barely pausing to kiss Zander's stomach before he had Zander's dick in his mouth.

A strangled cry filled the air. Zander's hips left the bed. Maverick felt powerful. Zander had more cock sucking skills than Maverick had ever encountered. Not only had Maverick not stopped thinking about the amazing blow job Zander had given him last night, he'd also been scared as hell he wouldn't measure up to Zander's porn star level abilities. Every sound Zander made had Maverick walking on clouds. Zander moaned and writhed like he was on camera, but the way he leaked in Maverick's mouth let him know it was all real. Goddamn. No one made him feel the way Zander did. His dick twitched like it was the one getting sucked while his pride soared. He fought the urge to beat his chest. Zander fucked him hard. Maverick put everything he had into pleasing Zander. He licked, sucked, tightened his throat, and hollowed out his cheeks. Saliva coated his hands, giving him a bit of lubricant to play with Zander's asshole.

He wanted to be inside Zander. The temptation to slam his way inside grew by the second. Then, Zander's body tensed, and Maverick forgot about everything else but stealing Zander's orgasm. Male salt coated his tongue. Maverick wanted more.

He loved the way Zander tasted. His tongue swiped Zander's crown, seeking more of the delicious pre-cum. He closed his lips around the head of Zander's cock and sucked. A cry bounced off the walls as cum exploded inside his mouth. Maverick moaned his pleasure as he lapped up every drop. Zander's dick was so damn pretty and tasted like heaven. Only Maverick's aching cock was enough to pull him away.

He leaned over the edge of the bed and found his condoms and lube before covering Zander's body once more. Zander didn't hesitate to bury his hands in Maverick's hair and pull him down for a kiss. Fuck, he loved a man who searched for the flavor of his own cum in a kiss. Tonight was about making love. He'd promised. But Maverick loved the idea of Zander getting dirty with him too. For now, he just needed to connect them. He needed Zander to feel something for him.

Zander pushed him away and tore open a condom. Maverick sat back on his heels. He watched as Zander rolled the sheath down Maverick's length. It was the hottest moment of his life and Maverick had no idea why. Something about the way Zander held his bottom lip between his teeth while handling Maverick's cock was fucking with his head. Zander coated the outside of the condom with lube. His gaze lifted, colliding with Maverick's. A roar of possessiveness swelled in Maverick's chest.

"I want you for more than one night. This isn't sex."

"I know."

"Do you?" Maverick asked, sounding calmer than he felt.

Zander stroked Maverick's cock. "Prove it."

He would. After he had Zander, he would keep coming back, sending flowers, and trying to shove his way into Zander's life. For now, Zander was right, all Maverick could do was prove himself.

He massaged Zander's thighs, urging them apart, making room for his large frame. Zander didn't hesitate to draw his legs up, welcoming him. Even Zander's asshole was sexy—like he was perfectly kept in every way. Maverick's was so turned on, even his thoughts were sounding insane. He positioned his crown at Zander's asshole. Their gazes never wavered. Maverick inched his way inside. Zander's hips left the bed, meeting him. Maverick slowly lowered his head. Their lips met. For a moment, they clung. Maverick's heart raced. Zander made set him on fire. He touched Maverick's heart. His throat burned from the intensity.

Zander's mouth opened over Maverick's bottom lip. Maverick's hips moved, slowly rocking against Zander. Fuck. He was amazing. The sounds Zander made were sexy as hell. If he hadn't swallowed Zander's cum minutes earlier, he would've thought Zander was ready to explode again. Maverick changed angles, deepening their kiss as he edged closer to release. He wanted to stay inside Zander all night. There was something happening between them. It grew alongside Maverick's pleasure. A sexy gasp vibrated around Maverick's tongue. Hot cum filled the space between them, taking Maverick by surprise and triggering his orgasm. His thoughts scattered as his body shook. Wave after wave rocked him. He couldn't stop pumping inside Zander. Even once he was spent, he was mentally aroused beyond reason.

"I want to keep making love to you all night, even when I'm no longer hard. All I want to do is keep stroking you and trying to get closer." Maverick wanted to bite his tongue and stop the words from flowing. There was no stemming the tidal wave. "Stay with me. Let me learn all your body's secrets."

"Okay." The quietly spoken agreement was all the permission Maverick needed. He took control of Zander's lips once more. Later, he'd wash the mess from their skin and explore every inch of Zander's body with his tongue. For now, he wanted Zander's kiss. That was all. Even though he didn't know why, Maverick felt complete when their lips touched.

CHAPTER 4

HE WASN'T THERE. ZANDER'S usual seat was empty. Maverick didn't know how to feel. It seemed, since they'd slept together, the bloom had fallen off the flower. Goddamn it. He'd told himself he wouldn't get attached. Zander probably wouldn't hang around. In truth, Maverick should've known it would be immediate. Zander was leagues above him. Making Zander chase him didn't make Maverick special. There was nothing about Maverick that made him stand out. He certainly didn't have anything to offer. Doubly so since he was now unemployed. Yep. That's how his day was going. He'd known there'd been talks of cutbacks for a few months now. Never in Maverick's wildest dreams had he expected to walk into work this morning and no longer have a job. Lowest man on the totem pole and all that since everyone else had been there for a hundred years.

Maverick tore his gaze away from Zander's empty seat. It was for the best that he lost Zander now before Maverick got attached. He ignored the tiny voice in his head, telling him it was too late. Zander already had him ensnared.

Rules were read. A bell rang. Maverick went through the motions. The dude got a shot in on Maverick's left eye. He could feel it swelling but no pain penetrated his haze. Somehow, Maverick managed a quick knockout, ending the match before Maverick was ready to face the sight of Zander's empty chair again. Still, even as his arms were raised in victory, Maverick's gaze slid that way. No blue eyes waited for him there. It was one hit too many for one day.

As he showered and changed, Maverick decided he needed to go out. He'd locked his life down a while back when he'd gotten tired of the party scene. Maybe it was time he got back out there. The last thing he needed was to go home alone with his thoughts tonight. Zander was still too fresh there. His expensive cologne and delicious body was still imprinted in Maverick's brain. His scent lingered on Maverick's sheets.

He made his way down the packed hallway, intent on making it to his truck with his sanity intact. Someone said his name. Maverick turned. Hope rose in his chest. His gaze landed on an unfamiliar set of gray eyes. The dude was hot, but not his hottie. Maverick didn't have to look down to meet his stare. That was new. Maverick rarely met anyone his height. The guy held out his hand.

"Maverick, I'm Jude Green with Green's Fighter Fuel. If you have a few minutes, I'd like to talk about sponsoring you to fight the legal circuit."

In Maverick's surprise, he shook Jude's hand a few moments too long. When he realized what he was doing, he quickly dropped the man's hand. "Sorry. Um, sure." He glanced around, looking for a quieter place to speak. His gaze landed on the same elevator he'd taken to go to dinner with Zander. He motioned toward it. "Would you like to head upstairs to the restaurant? It might be quieter up there."

Jude's gaze moved toward the elevator. "Isn't there a coffee shop up there, as well? How about we do that instead?"

Maverick nodded and led the way. He fought the urge to glance behind him. Green's Fighter Fuel wasn't unknown to him. They were one of Zeke's sponsors. Maverick never, ever expected this. His disbelief had him automatically looking for loopholes the second they were seated inside the mostly empty coffee shop.

"You realize I'm in the same weight class as Zeke Armstrong, right? Don't you already sponsor him?"

Jude had a nice smile, and if Maverick wasn't mistaken, he was silently laughing at Maverick's reaction. "I'm aware, but you're close to the line. If you're willing to put on five pounds, you could go up a weight class."

Maverick nodded, trying damn hard not to look as ignorant as he felt. "I don't think that'll be a problem, but I've never fought on the circuit."

"That's not an issue. You already train with the right people. It's not that different. Only more structured. You fight only the matches we approve. Matches that benefit us and move you closer to winning a title. Obviously, you should speak with a lawyer, and think things over.

There's no way you can work a day job and do this. Training for a title is a full-time job."

Maverick tried to swallow back his excitement. He fought not to admit he'd just been let go from his job. Instead, he nodded while trying to look thoughtful and not at all overwhelmed. "I'm not independently wealthy, so…"

Jude's smile was laughing at him again. It struck Maverick once more how handsome the guy was. He was wide shouldered with a massive chest. Jude looked close to forty-five with his graying scruff and bald head. Jude Green was a sexy bear.

"If you accept our deal and start winning matches in the circuit like you have been in bet fights, you'll never have to worry over money again."

And Zander wouldn't be out of his reach any longer. Maverick couldn't stop that thought from intruding. Still, Maverick didn't want to appear as floored as he was. "Like you said, I'll have to consult my lawyer."

"Perfect. Let's make plans to meet after you've had time to think things over and talk more about it."

"Sounds good," Maverick said, digging out his phone so he could save Jude's number to his contact list. Zander's name stared up at him from an unread message. Maverick's thoughts stumbled. Everything else could wait. He quickly opened his messages.

Zander: *I'm so sorry. I'll have to miss your match tonight. A problem cropped up at my Vegas location. May I see you when I get back?*

Maverick couldn't fight his smile. His gaze lifted and collided with serious gray eyes. The way Jude watched him wasn't necessarily comfortable.

"You should give me your number."

Maverick didn't respond. There was something dark in Jude's tone.

"So we can schedule a meeting," Jude clarified, soothing Maverick's unease.

"Of course," Maverick said, rattling off his number while feeling like an idiot. Jude had just made him the offer of a lifetime. His unease seemed ridiculous.

Zander spun his cellphone in his hands. Maverick hadn't responded to his text. Maybe one night with Zander was enough. After all, Zander had fourteen years on Maverick. Maverick didn't seem to give a damn about Zander's money. Of course, then again, Maverick wouldn't be the first to play that game.

A growl rose in Zander's throat. He was half a second away from chucking his phone when it buzzed. In his surprise, he juggled the device for a moment before getting his messages open.

Maverick: *When can I expect this mystery visit?*

Zander had to take a deep breath to fight off the possessiveness rising inside him. He scared himself when it came to Maverick. Zander was afraid of how far he'd go to keep him.

Zander: *I'll be home in the morning.*

Maverick: *I don't usually fight back-to-back nights, but I am this weekend. Can I see you afterward?*

Zander: *I'll be there.*

He lasted all of five seconds before he decided their short text exchange wasn't enough.

Zander: *Can I see you sooner than that?*

He bit his lip, wondering if his desperation peeked through. From what he understood that wasn't attractive.

Zander: *Maybe I could take you to breakfast.*

Zander: *Unless you have to work.*

He barely stopped himself from covering his eyes. Even to him, he was starting to sound like an idiot. Zander considered sitting on his hands to keep from sending out anymore texts.

Maverick: *What are your plans for tonight?*

Zander: *Nothing. I just can't charter a plane until the morning.*

He was back to waiting. It was torture waiting for each text to roll in.

Maverick: *Okay. I called my sister. She works for Western Air. If you want, and I can crash with you and ride back with you, I could come to you tonight. *hopeful face**

"You must be talking to Maverick. That's the only time you smile like that."

Zander's head snapped up at Yaro's observation. "Yes. He's flying in to see me."

Yaro and Pytor exchanged a smile and left him alone. He didn't care if those fools thought he was ridiculous. They'd seen him in much more humiliating positions than being happy for once.

Zander: *I would love that. Let me know the ticket price and I'll pay, since you're coming to see me.*

Maverick: *I wouldn't have offered if I wasn't willing to pay. Don't think about the money. Just let me enjoy coming to be with you. I'll be there by ten.*

Fuck. It drove him crazy that Maverick wouldn't let him do anything for him. But Maverick was right, as long as they were together, Zander couldn't fuss about money.

Zander: *Okay. Can't wait to see you.*

Maverick: *Same.*

Zander stood and paced. He fought the urge to crack a bottle of vodka to kill time. His skin felt too tight. He was like an addict, itching for his next high.

"Come on," Yaro said, pulling him from his impatience. He motioned to–

ward the door when Zander looked his way. "Let's go grab some food and then wait at the airport for your man. Otherwise, you're likely to wear a hole in the floor."

Zander damn near raced to the door. Over the next three hours, Zander had never been more thankful for his guards. They kept him busy, ensuring he didn't climb the walls. Every second of suffering was worth the moment Maverick crawled into the backseat with him and overcame him, covering his mouth with his as if they were alone. Pytor turned up the radio to give them as much privacy as possible.

"Why is your eye swollen and black?" Zander asked between kisses. "Did you throw another match?"

Maverick chuckled against his lips. "I won. Your empty seat just distracted me a little."

Zander groaned. "Oh no. I tried to text you before your match."

"I missed it somehow. It's been a hell of a day." Maverick sat close with his arms wrapped around Zander. It was like being wrapped in heaven.

His whole body sang. "I'm here to listen."

"Do you get driven everywhere?"

Zander wondered if Maverick didn't want to tell him about his day. "I don't drive. What happened today?"

"Like never?" Maverick asked.

"No."

Maverick seemed unnaturally fascinated by the revelation. "You don't, or you can't?"

Zander shrugged. "I never learned. Why was your day bad?"

"I could teach you."

"For the love of God, why was your day bad?" Zander asked with a laugh.

Maverick blew out a sigh. "Well, it wasn't completely bad. I'm here now, and I got offered a sponsorship to fight the legal circuit."

"That's amazing."

"I also got let go from my job," Maverick added, saving the bad news for last.

"Holy shit. Are you kidding me? You should've called."

Maverick's sexy smile was everything. "What would you have done? Bought the firehouse?"

Zander held back his eye roll by force of will alone. "I would've listened to you vent."

"It's okay." Maverick brought Zander's hand to his lips. His tiny kisses tickled the back of Zander's hand. "I'm with you now."

Once his inner slut finished cooing, his business side took over. "If you no longer have a job, why wouldn't you let me pay for your plane ticket? Surely you need to keep your money more than ever right now."

Maverick's heated gaze almost made Zander forget to be pragmatic. "I'll worry over that later. Tonight, I have this," he said, claiming Zander's mouth again. Maverick made life sound so easy—like he could live on Zander's kisses alone. He had no idea how his sweet treatment completely wrecked Zander.

CHAPTER 5

IT WAS POSSIBLE THAT waiting for
Maverick outside the locker room
smacked a bit too close to desperation. Zander didn't care. It was getting harder to stay away. He'd been
stalking Maverick too long—watching and wanting. Now that Maverick
was his, Zander resented every second they spent apart.

With his hair still dripping from his
shower and gym bag in hand, Maverick stepped into the hallway. His gaze

found Zander's like they were connected. The way Maverick's mouth lifted in the corner the instant he spotted Zander had Zander sucking in a sharp breath. Maverick wasn't ashamed of whatever he felt for Zander. That was more than obvious by the way he closed the distance between them. Yaro and Pytor shifted positions, turning their backs, and doing their best to hide Maverick and him from sight as Maverick overcame him. Their lips met. For the first time all day, Zander drew a steady breath. It was odd how nothing felt right when Maverick wasn't around. As always, when they kissed, Maverick turned dominant. His fingers dug into Zander's jaw, controlling their pace. Everything else about Maverick was gentle, stealing Zander's heart. Maverick had no clue how his loving treatment was Zander's undoing—how no one else had ever been nice to him. He always unbalanced Zander.

"Goddamn," Maverick whispered against his lips, further melting Zander. "I've been waiting all day for that." Before Zander could respond in kind, Maverick deepened their kiss once more.

"Oh, I'm sorry," a male voice said, interrupting them.

Maverick's head shot up, but he didn't release Zander. His grip turned into a caress as they looked their intruder's way. A red-haired guy close to Maverick's age stared back at them. It took Zander a moment to place him. He was Maverick's corner man. They knew each other, but Zander couldn't remember his name.

"Hey, Hendrix. What's up?"

Hendrix. That was it. Zander barely stopped himself from snapping his fingers. The guy's unusually light green gaze moved between them. If Zander wasn't mistaken, there was some disapproval mixed with Hendrix's surprise. That was nothing new for Zander. He was used to everyone disapproving of him. It was doubly understandable coming from Hendrix. Their history wasn't good.

He held out an envelope to Maverick. "Your winnings."

"Thanks, man," Maverick said, reaching for the envelope. "I was headed to find you, but I got distract-ed."

Hendrix's gaze slid Zander's way once more. "I see that." After anoth-er scathing look at Zander, Hendrix switched his attention to Maverick. "Don't forget, I reserved the cage for two o'clock tomorrow. Zeke needs the practice."

Maverick nodded. "No worries. I'll be there."

With a nod, Hendrix walked away. Maverick didn't watch him go. He focused on Zander as if the corner man was already forgotten.

"What should we do now that we're all alone?" Maverick shook the envelope. His gaze never wavered from Zander. "I could take you out. Show you off. Make the world jealous that you'll be going home with me."

Damn. Maverick was amazing. "As much as that appeals to me, you should hang onto your money, and let me spoil you for once."

With a dramatic groan Maverick fell against the wall. "Ugh. You know how much I hate you spending your money."

Zander couldn't stop smiling. "You'll live through it for one night."

Maverick's expression transformed from playful to loving, stealing Zander's heart. He tucked Zander's hair behind his ear. "I know you don't understand, but I need to be the one person in your life who wants nothing from you except your time."

"You already are that person, so meet me halfway. I need to be the one person in your life who spoils you, even though you don't need me. Give me permission to do whatever I want for you for just one night. No complaining or regrets from you." He could practically feel Maverick wavering. Zander gave him one final push. "Please?"

Maverick's shoulders fell, and Zander knew he'd won. "One night."

Even though Maverick didn't know it yet, Zander was determined it would be one hell of a night.

Maverick relaxed in the center of Zander's bed, wondering if his bones could turn to jelly. Between Zander forcing him to shop half the night, pleasuring his body in the best of ways, and the sheer luxury of Zander's amazing bed, Maverick was useless.

A solid weight landed on Maverick. "I've been thinking."

Maverick took in the sexiness straddling his body. His hands lifted with no input from his brain. Zander's nude body was too much temptation to resist. No matter how many ways he'd already had Zander tonight. "Mhmm, you've been thinking," Maverick parroted as his fingers traced Zander's abs down to his cock. He watched it stir. Zander's skin was still damp from his shower. Maverick wanted to lick him.

CHARITY PARKERSON

"Yes. You should delay Green. Tell him your lawyer is backed up and can't get you in for a while. He's a businessman. That's an excuse he'll understand."

Maverick tried listening. There was too much beauty on his hips. "Why am I delaying Green?" Maverick palmed Zander's shaft as he asked the question. He loved feeling Zander go hard in his hand.

"Would you say I'm good at making money and know a lot about the sport?"

"Smartest man I know," Maverick agreed, stroking Zander's dick, and barely paying attention to his words.

Zander covered Maverick's hand with his, guiding him into a rhythm he liked. "Damn. That's good," Zander said, sounding breathless. "I think you should enter one circuit match without a sponsor and try for a bigger fish than Green before choosing to sign on with him."

Maverick froze. He met Zander's gaze. "That seems like kind of a shitty thing to do to Green after he made me an offer."

Zander shook his head. "You're too nice. This business will eat you alive. I'm not telling you to fuck him over. I'm suggesting you look out for your best interests. You're good. If you wanted, you could set yourself up for life with sponsors. You're allowed to have as many as you want, as long as they're not competing businesses. But if you go into your first circuit match already tied to someone, you might miss an even bigger deal. I'm not telling you not to sign with Green. Just let a few more people look at you before you settle on the first offer. If nothing else, Green might be willing to part with even more money if he sees a competitor is interested. Don't let him take you cheap. Going pro means being a businessman as well as a fighter."

Zander made sense. Plus, he was smart and would look out more for Maverick's interest than Green would. He went back to stroking Zander's cock with Zander helping. It was an awesome show. One that already had Maverick ready to fuck like they hadn't been all night. "So, you think these potential sponsors will just show up to a no-name fighter's match and start throwing money at me?"

Zander's hips moved against Maverick's fist. He threw his head back and gasped, stealing Maverick's thoughts. When his chin dropped, Zander's eyes were bright with lust. Still, he managed to hold a conversation. "Let me handle that. I'll make some calls and get some people there."

"People?"

Zander braced his palms on Maverick's shoulders and openly fucked Maverick's hands. He made it damn hard to concentrate. Zander was a twenty-four-seven porn channel Maverick didn't want to stop watching. "Maybe Left Hook Energy Drinks and Coastal Clean Eats."

Those were some huge names. Almost big enough to make Maverick forget what he was doing. "If you do that, I won't feel like I earned it."

A low moan escaped Zander. His voice came out in a pant. "Bullshit. You'll have to work for it. They won't just hand you a sponsorship. You'll have to earn it. I'm just getting them there. The rest is up to you. Goddamn. Do that again," Zander gasped when Maverick brushed his thumb along Zander's slit. They'd need to talk more about it and hammer out the details. But as Maverick pulled Zander down for a kiss, giving into his desire to fuck this gorgeous man, he knew he'd follow Zander's advice. He hadn't been flattering Zander earlier. Zander was the smartest person he knew. Maverick would be insane not to take advice about his financial future from a billionaire. Plus, whatever Zander wanted, it was his. Maverick was pretty sure the guy just owned him now.

Maverick was gone. The house felt devoid of life without him. All through his shower and getting dressed for the day, Zander fought a black mood that threatened to overcome him. He'd done so good lately. The dark days came less and less. Zander didn't want to fall into the hole today. He headed for his office, searching for his phone. Maybe he'd send Maverick a text. The thought alone already had his mood lightening. A smile stretched his lips. He'd dropped so much money on Maverick in a matter of hours last night, Maverick's horror had been almost tangible. Holding to their agreement, Maverick hadn't complained not once.

Since Maverick had lost his job, Zander did some practical things for him, as well. He hoped the gesture would stop Maverick from resenting Zander too much when his one night of spoiling Maverick was over. He'd bought him groceries. Paid his rent for the next six months. An evil laugh escaped Zander at the memory of Maverick's expression over that one. He'd been biting his tongue damn hard. Zander was surprised he hadn't bitten it off. The thing was, Zander would've found a way to do all those things for Maverick anyhow. It was better for Maverick to agree. Of course, Zander was certain Maverick hadn't known exactly how far Zander would go. He needed to slow down. The last thing he wanted was to scare Maverick away.

A folded piece of paper, underneath Zander's cellphone on his desk, caught his eye. Zander unfolded the letter. Seeing Maverick's name brought an immediate smile to Zander's face without reading anything else. Zander sat before pouring over every word.

Zander,

You looked so goddamn sexy sleeping, I couldn't wake you. Now that I'm set to leave, it's killing me I didn't get *to kiss you goodbye. I'm pretty sure you own me. Not because of anything tangible. It's damn sure not because of the fucking money you spent on me last night. I said I wouldn't bitch. I didn't say I wouldn't pout. Anyhow, it's just you that's wowed me. All I want to do anymore is be with you. Unfortunately, we each have things we have to do, pulling us in different directions. **sad face** But I'll miss you today. I can already tell it'll be a long day without you. Ugh, now I wonder if you'll think I sound desperate. Toss this in the trash if you think I'm ridiculous and we'll pretend this never happened. Otherwise, text me when you wake up, so I can tell you good morning.*

XOXO,

Maverick

Zander chewed his bottom lip, trying to fight a smile that wouldn't abate. Maverick was adorable. He over-thought everything. Maverick made Zander want to protect that spark inside Maverick that made him leave notes and send flowers. He deserved only good things. Maverick did so many nice things for Zander. Flowers and notes were only a small part of what Maverick gave Zander simply by existing. Zander wanted to be the same, but he didn't know how. If it involved money, Maverick would resent it, even though Zander refused to stop trying to give Maverick gifts.

"You have a meeting soon. We should leave."

Zander stared at Pytor at the announcement, unmoving.

Pytor's eyebrows rose. "Are you okay?"

Zander nodded. "I'd like to do something nice for Maverick, but I don't know what." He caught himself trying to blush, but Pytor had been with him long enough embarrassment was ridiculous.

Pytor dropped, filling the center of Zander's office couch, dwarfing the large piece. "Huh. Well, he lives in a tiny apartment. You could buy him a house."

A bright smile snapped to Zander's lips. "Think smaller. I dropped some money on him last night and it made him cranky."

"He makes you smile. This one deserves a big gift," Pytor said, sounding confused.

Love swelled in Zander's chest for this sweet man who'd been watching over Zander for the past twenty-two years. They were friends. He knew he could count on Pytor for anything, but his longtime guard and friend probably couldn't help him with this. Still, Zander didn't give up. "Maverick isn't like me. He isn't swayed by money. It'll take a small gesture, but a sweet one to win him over. I don't know how to do that."

"Well, you wouldn't know how to do that, would you?" Pytor said, sounding serious. "After the way Gio treated you, and all that. And, by the way, you're not swayed by money either. You might be a shrewd businessman, but no one has ever touched your heart by buying you things. This guy, he's nice to you. I like it."

"You should send him a card," Yaro said from the doorway, shamelessly listening. "He's already sent you flowers, so you can't copy him. My papa used to give my mama a card every Friday. She had boxes and boxes of them. I don't know what they said, but my parents loved each other very much. They were poor but happy."

Pytor nodded. "That could work. They also had ten kids, so they obviously couldn't keep their hands off each other."

"That's my mama you're talking about," Yaro said, looking outraged. Pytor and Yaro had grown up together and fought like brothers. Only Zander truly understood their relationship. They were the family Zander didn't have.

Zander didn't hesitate to jump in to tease Yaro as well. "They were too poor to afford birth control, so..."

Instead of adding fuel to Yaro's fire, he looked defeated. "This is true. They used to use my papa's socks for condoms, but all papa's socks had holes in them."

It didn't matter if Yaro was being serious, the result was the same. A burst of laughter exploded from Zander, surprising him. He slapped his hand over his mouth to no avail. He couldn't stop. It didn't help that both men stared at him like he was insane.

Yaro shook his head. "You'll buy a card and I'll deliver it. This guy makes you happy. If you've ever laughed, I can't remember it. You'll keep this one. We'll help."

Zander swiped at his eyes. He couldn't deny it. Everything about Maverick lit Zander from the inside. Zander couldn't let Maverick get away.

While waiting for his reserved cage time, Maverick warmed up. Hendrix sat nearby watching and giving pointers.

"I noticed last night you kept dropping your right shoulder. You can't have that sort of tell if you want to keep winning."

Maverick nodded and concentrated on not dropping his shoulder before going in for a few quick jabs.

"I was surprised to see you with Zander Kapra of all people last night," Hendrix said, catching Maverick off guard by broaching the topic. Usually, Hendrix never said anything about anyone Maverick dated.

Maverick spun, landing a spin kick on the bag. "Why? You think I'm not good enough to land someone like him? It's not like you to have an opinion on things like that."

The way Hendrix's gaze skirted away set alarms clanging in Maverick's head. "Nah. I've seen you in action. You can have anyone you want. It's just that I've always thought of you as the shining armor type."

"Okay," Maverick said, dragging out the word. "I have no idea what that's supposed to mean, but whatever."

Hendrix shrugged. "It's not a big deal. You just hear things, you know?" Maverick didn't know, but Hendrix didn't make him say as much. "I mean, he needs full-time protection following him around for a reason."

"Yeah. He's rich."

Hendrix snorted. "So is just about everyone you meet around here, but you don't see them with Russian security. Never mind, man. I was just thinking aloud."

Maverick had no idea what the nationality of Zander's guards had to do with anything. Still, if Hendrix wanted to drop it, Maverick was cool with that.

Except, he didn't let it go. "I mean, I guess I thought you were better than letting some rich guy who could make or break your career buy you."

Maverick dropped his arms and gave Hendrix his attention. "He hasn't bought me. We're seeing each other. I like him. He likes me. That's all there is to it."

Hendrix didn't look like he believed Maverick. "Aren't you worried people will question your every win now? Can you honestly say if you get offered a big sponsorship, you'll feel like you earned it?"

"Yes. I can honestly say that I earned it because I've worked damn hard for years without Zander around. Plus, I've made it more than clear that our relationship has to be separate from my career or we can't be together. He's made no attempt to interfere. It's all good."

"All right," Hendrix said, obviously intent on really letting it go this time. "If you have things under control, that's cool."

With a nod, Maverick went back to his warm up. Hendrix went back to handing out pointers. All discussion of Zander disappeared. Still, by the time he finished sparring with Zeke, he was damn ready to get out from underneath Hendrix's disapproving stare. He didn't understand what the guy's problem was with Zander, but he was already tired of the silent accusations in Hendrix's eyes. All the money he'd let Zander drop on him last night wasn't helping Maverick's mood. It gave Hendrix's claim a tiny bit of credence. Fuck, Maverick almost wished he could go back and tell Zander he couldn't spoil him. Almost. Zander's expression, though. That had made every sting to his pride worth it. He'd never seen Zander happier.

When the outside air hit the sweat on Maverick's skin, he nearly sighed in relief. He was ready to get home. At least, that's what he told himself to save his pride. In truth, the need to get back to Zander was crippling. There was a card tucked beneath Maverick's windshield wiper. Maverick tossed his gym bag inside his truck before grabbing the red envelope. He didn't open it until he was behind the wheel. A picture of a dancing elephant in a yellow tutu stared up at him. Maverick opened the card.

Maverick,

I spent way too much time trying to figure out why this card had a dancing elephant on it, but I like it. The elephant reminds me of how I feel inside most of the time—on display and ridiculous. Since I met you, I've been happy. I don't want it to stop. I thought, if you're worried over leaving me a letter, we'd overthink things together, and I'd leave you one too. You should've woken me this morning. One kiss from you is worth more than any amount of sleep. Now that I've missed that goodbye kiss, my day is out of sync. Nothing feels right. You must fix this. Tomorrow, I expect two kisses to make up for today. Text me when you are free. We'll make plans to make it happen.

XOXO,

Zander

Maverick couldn't stop smiling. Hendrix's claims muted in the back of his mind. Zander was the greatest guy Maverick had met in a long damn time. He wouldn't let anyone ruin that by getting in his head. Without an ounce of hesitation, Maverick dug his phone out of his bag, and sent off a text to Zander.

Maverick: *I need a shower, but I'm free.*

He expected to have to wait until after he was home to see a response to his text since he knew Zander had several meetings today. To his surprise, his phone immediately vibrated with an incoming message.

Zander: *There are showers at my house, and clothes since you let me spoil you.*

Despite being alone, with no one to witness his shame over how much money Zander had spent on him last night, Maverick still groaned.

Maverick: *But there's no you at your house.*

Zander: *That's not true in the least. My last two meetings are phone conferences. I'm handling those at home. Once those are done, and you've enjoyed all my hot water, we'll be free to do whatever you like.*

Fuck it. Maverick didn't give two shits what anyone thought. He knew the truth. They were headed to a full-blown future together. Maverick felt it in his bones. This wasn't some mutual benefit shit. Maverick felt something for Zander. He wanted to spend every free minute with the guy. If that meant showering at Zander's house and wearing clothes he hadn't paid for, then that's what he'd do to get five more minutes with Zander.

Maverick: *On my way.*

Zander: *I'll let Pytor know to keep an eye out. BTW, I've missed you today.*

Maverick smiled like an idiot as he read Zander's text. Jesus, he had it bad. Zander possessed something no one else did. Maverick couldn't get enough.

Maverick: *I've missed you too. When I get there, I'm getting those missed kisses, and thanking you properly for my card.*

Zander: *I can't wait.*

Neither could Maverick. That's why he tossed his phone aside and fired his truck to life. He still had lots and lots of things to say, but he wanted to say all of it in person.

Zander stared at his hands. His final conference call had wound down fifteen minutes ago, but he hadn't moved. He flattened his palms on the desk. This had been Gio's desk. Why hadn't he burned it? Each breath came harder than the last. Zander fucking hated moments like this. They always struck when he least expected, knocking the air from his lungs. He blinked, trying to hold back the tide. If the blackness swept him under, he might not come back this time. Everything felt off. What was he supposed to be doing?

"Pytor said you were finished for the day. Is it okay if I come in?"

Zander's head shot up. Maverick stood in the doorway, wearing nothing except a pair of workout shorts. He looked unsure of his welcome. Light burst through the darkness inside Zander's head. A smile pulled at his lips. "Of course. I was just about to come looking for you."

Maverick crossed the room. While wearing a bright smile, he pulled Zander's chair away from the desk, and dropped to his knees at Zander's feet. He wrapped his arms around Zander's waist, pressed his forehead to Zander's chest and held on. Zander held him. Maverick had no idea how much Zander needed this. Just this.

Someone who cared about him, holding him.

"You make me weak," Maverick said almost too quiet to hear.

A smile touched Zander's lips. "Funny. You make me strong."

Maverick tilted his chin up and met Zander's stare. "Is it okay if I ask you something?"

Zander didn't hesitate. "I'm always at your disposal."

"Why do you always have security with you?" Maverick asked, surprising Zander with his odd question. He'd expected almost anything except that. "I mean, you can't turn around in this town without tripping over someone richer than God, but you're one of the few with a security team."

There was something in Maverick's tone. Zander tried diffusing it. He flashed Maverick a smile. "You should know by now that Yaro and Pytor or more like family than security. They came with me from Russia. This is their home. This is the only job they've ever known. One of the biggest reasons I don't bother learning to drive is to save Yaro's pride. He would feel like he had a pity job if I didn't need him." Maverick chewed his bottom lip. Zander's stomach growled. He wanted to kiss away whatever was eating at Maverick. "What is it?"

Maverick's lips curved into a sexy smile. "It's nothing." The way Maverick's eyes flashed with mischief had Zander's stomach muscles clenching. He massaged Zander's thighs while biting his lip and eyeing Zander like he didn't know where to start. Zander would take anything Maverick was willing to give him. Even if Maverick only offered a kiss, Zander wanted it. "Goddamn. You make me feel like the luckiest man."

Sometimes, Maverick left him speechless. Most people would take one look at Zander and assume he had everything. Having Maverick made him feel as if he'd never had a damn thing before now—like blessings rained down on his head.

"You could ask for anything right now," Zander said past his tight throat. Maverick owned him more than he would ever know. Anything Maverick wanted, it was his.

"Is that so?" Maverick's teasing tone had Zander going hard. He popped two buttons loose on Zander's shirt. "How about this shirt?" Maverick slid two more buttons loose. "Can I have it?"

"It's not really your color," Zander said, trying for a bland tone and hoping to keep Maverick entertained.

Maverick held his stare as he stole Zander's shirt. "Then we should get rid of it." Maverick tossed it aside.

All Zander could do was hold the arms of the chair in a death grip and stare as Maverick leaned in and licked his stomach. He sucked in a hiss as Maverick's tongue stroked the skin at the edge of his pants.

Maverick's nimble fingers made quick work of Zander's belt. The button on his pants loosened. Maverick slowly slid his zipper down.

Zander needed to see Maverick's eyes. He cupped Maverick's chin, leaving him no choice but to look at him. For a moment, the world went still as they stared at each other. Zander had been obsessed with Maverick for so long. It shouldn't have shocked him how much emotion rose in his chest at that moment, but it did. He cared more about Maverick than he did anyone. His gaze moved over Maverick's face, taking in his flushed cheeks and labored breaths. He wanted Zander as much as Zander wanted him. It was... moving—like Maverick would've chosen him no matter who he was. No one else made him feel that way.

He couldn't let Maverick's expression turn to hate. Zander needed to ensure Maverick never stopped looking at him this way. "Tell me why you're upset. I can see you trying to make light of whatever is happening inside your head." It was true. Maverick acted the way Zander did when he needed to hide his fear. As much as he craved everything Maverick promised with his heated stares, Zander needed Maverick's happiness even more. "You can always talk to me."

Maverick stroked Zander's thighs in a nervous gesture that punched Zander in the chest. "It's nothing, really." He licked his lips. "This guy at the gym, he said some shit and got in my head. I shouldn't have let it bother me."

Zander released Maverick's chin. "If he said you can do better than an old man, he's right, but I'm not giving you up." Even though Zander laughed as he made the claim, he didn't feel it.

Maverick shook his head and dipped his chin. He swiped his tongue down Zander's stomach. "Not only are you not old, you're also twice as hot as anyone my age, so fuck all that noise." Zander's laughter turned genuine until Maverick's next words killed it. "He said I'll never win another fight without everyone wondering if it's because of you. If I get any sponsorships, it'll always be in the back of my mind that I didn't earn them, and that I should question why you need security. Basically, it was insinuated that you're not a good person and I'm bought and paid for already."

The rage, it was real. Zander wanted to demand this man's name and have his entire existence scrubbed from the planet. He took a breath, hoping to calm his temper. Zander should've expected this sooner. People talked. Right now, Maverick needed reassurance. Not Zander's temper.

He pasted on a smile he didn't feel and stroked Maverick's face. "Sexy, you know damn well you've earned every good thing coming your way. You had a ninety-five percent win ratio before you ever met me. I'm not the one in that cage winning matches.

That's you. All you. Don't let anyone steal that from you with their bitterness. As far as sponsors go, you already know how I feel about all that. But you won Green all by yourself. If you want to call Jude right now and accept his offer just to prove to yourself you don't need me, then do it." His smile turned genuine as he saw the doubt clear from Maverick's eyes. "All I want is for you to be happy. Setting you in front of bigger sponsors is not buying you. I can't force them to offer you lots of money. You have to earn that on your own." He leaned forward and kissed Maverick's nose. "I only pressed you to go for bigger fish because I believe in you," Zander said, touching his forehead to Maverick's and holding his stare. "You don't need me at all."

Maverick's arms locked around Zander's waist. His expression turned devious. "I don't know about that," he said, hauling Zander from the chair and falling backward. "I'm feeling pretty damn needy right now."

Zander braced his palms on the floor next to Maverick's head. He lowered his weight until his lips brushed Maverick's in the lightest kiss. Every day he felt closer to Maverick. He didn't know how to process how Maverick made him feel. Neither could he make Maverick understand why everything he did for Zander mattered so much. Instead of trying to find the right words, Zander brushed another light kiss across Maverick's lips before moving to his jaw, and then his neck. He felt Maverick swallow.

Maverick cupped his face and held him away. "I never, ever want you to think I'm here for any reason other than I want to be with you. If you ever, for even one minute, think I want a cent of your money, it would kill me. Promise me you don't believe that."

Zander took a deep breath, trying to control the possessiveness rising inside him. Maverick would never understand, Zander didn't give a fuck if he was there for the money. He could have it all. "I promise."

Maverick shoved both hands down the back of Zander's open pants. He squeezed and massaged Zander's ass. The need to act overtook Zander. There weren't powerful enough words to describe the emotions welling inside him. Thankfully, Maverick only wore shorts. Zander tore at them.

"I need you to fuck me. Hard. Don't hold back."

At Zander's plea, Maverick went still beneath him. "Are you sure?"

Was he insane? "Yes. Now."

In a flash, Maverick was on his feet with Zander thrown over one shoulder. A moan rose and stuck in his throat over Maverick's show of strength. His long stride carried them to the bedroom. At the edge of the bed, Maverick set him on his feet and stripped away their clothes. He heard something rip. Zander didn't give a fuck. His cock leaked at the sound. Maverick was about to give him what he needed. That's all his body knew. That's all that mattered. He felt drunk with anticipation.

Once they were nude, Maverick kissed him deep, stealing Zander's breath before he found himself bent over the bed with his face buried in the mattress. Cool liquid swiped his asshole. Slick fingers stretched him wide. Zander fought the urge to grind his hips against the bed, taking his pleasure from the mattress. Maverick's dick replaced his fingers. Zander bit down on the comforter to hold in his cries as Maverick roughly shoved his way inside. Once fully seated, Maverick changed angles and pounded him. Each stroke was hard and deep. He pulled Zander's hair, yanking his head back and holding on as he lifted Zander off his feet with each thrust. Zander couldn't think. All he could do was feel. Maverick hit at the perfect angle, massaging that spot inside him that brought him so much pleasure. Zander tasted blood. Only then did he realize he'd been biting his lip to keep from screaming Maverick's name.

Maverick's teeth sank into his back. "Is this what you wanted? Or do you need more?"

"Yes." Dear god. Even Zander didn't know what he begged for. All he knew was Maverick would give it to him.

Maverick pulled out, scooped Zander's feet from the floor, and tossed him onto the bed. He dug through the draw where Zander kept his toys. There was no embarrassment. Only need. Maverick joined him on the bed and shoved his thighs apart. Zander stared at his hard face. A wave of relief washed over him. Maverick understood. He had what Zander needed. This man would never shame him for being twisted. They were the same.

More lube coated his ass. This time, when Maverick pushed his way inside, he eased in. Zander gasped at the huge intrusion. Maverick's cock and Zander's favorite dildo were shoving their way inside. Maverick kept his gaze locked on his hands, concentrating on his task. Zander tasted more blood. He wouldn't beg.

"Hurt me." Fuck. He couldn't stop.

Maverick's gaze shot to his. There was no hiding his desperation. Zander knew Maverick could see it written in his every line. "Fuck your hand," Maverick ordered, sounding stern. "Do you remember that first blow job you gave me? Do that with your hand? If you come before you've built up at least three orgasms, I swear I'll stop."

Zander nodded. He couldn't let Maverick stop. His fingers encircled his cock. He was already so close to the edge. Obviously satisfied Zander would comply, Maverick pushed Zander's thighs open even wider. He positioned the dildo deep enough it wouldn't slip away, held it in place and thrust. The moment Maverick's hips slapped his ass, Zander almost came. He squeezed his dick, cutting off the first orgasm. The move almost blinded him. He didn't think

he'd ever been so desperate for release, but he didn't want Maverick
to stop. When the insanity passed,
Zander started jacking off again. He
was a master at giving pleasure. To
himself and others. Maverick fucked
him hard, filling him to capacity in
a painful way that was pleasure.
Tomorrow, he'd feel this and think
of Maverick. He'd get hot and touch
himself. Pressure beat at his crown
at the idea of what tomorrow would
bring. He'd sneak away, find his toys,
and try to recreate what Maverick
did for him. Maybe Zander would dig
out the rubber ass he owned, lube it,
and pretend Maverick let him do the
same things to his ass. This time,
Zander almost slipped. His need was

too great. He choked off the second orgasm. This time, it almost didn't work. Between Maverick pounding him and the dirty images in his head. Zander was too turned on. It took longer for the storm to pass before he could stroke himself once more.

"That's it," Maverick praised, sounding strained. "Come for me this time. Threaten to break me with your tight asshole clamping down in release. Suck me off with your spasms."

Zander tugged and strained. His fist moved faster and faster, pumping him toward oblivion. The sound of skin slapping skin mixed with the perfection of how Maverick fucked him. Tomorrow, he'd see how Maverick would let him push him. Test the waters. Maybe, tomorrow, he'd be the one fucking Maverick. Ecstasy slammed into Zander, tearing Maverick's name from his lips. His entire body went into lockdown as wave after wave rocked him, stealing his breath and sight. He couldn't stop tugging on his cock, reaching for more. It went on and on until Zander was nothing more than sensation. Maverick collapsed, molding against him. Zander fought the urge to scream. His nerves were too sensitive. They felt too perfect. He couldn't think straight. He pulled at Maverick's hair, urging Maverick's mouth to his. Zander licked and sucked, trying to take everything from him. It wasn't enough. Zander pulled him closer and sank his teeth into Maverick's earlobe. "One day, I'll fuck you. You'll let me. It'll be fucking perfect and you'll scream my name."

"Goddamn," Maverick whispered sounding winded. "I can't wait."

Maverick awoke on a gasp. Even he didn't understand what had ripped him from the deepest of sleeps. After the way Zander had worked out his body, he would've expected to pass out for days. The bed was empty. The house was dark. Maverick padded from room to empty room, searching for Zander. Each time he came to a closed door, he debated whether he should open it. From what he gathered, Yaro and Pytor lived there as well. The last thing he wanted was to stumble upon either of them in the nude. Maverick didn't imagine they'd appreciate it.

With the second floor searched, Maverick hit the stairs and checked the obvious places first. The kitchen and living room were both devoid of life. He passed a hallway and the screech of hardcore metal music floated out. Maverick followed the sound. The hallway opened up into a huge room that made Maverick's jaw drop. The ceiling was as high as all three floors put together, obviously taking up one entire end of the house. There were climbing rocks, hanging hooks, and water hazards. It was a full-blown ninja training center slash parkour course.

Music blared from unseen speakers. Pytor stood shirtless with his hands on his hips and staring upward. Once Maverick managed to tear his eyes away from the deep, long scars across Pytor's back, Maverick followed the guard's gaze to the wall. First, he spotted Zander. Wearing nothing but shorts, not even shoes, he scaled a wall that had water flowing down the side. Each muscle strained, standing out for Maverick's inspection. Maverick's mouth watered.

"Come on, Yaro. You can't let him win again. This is a matter of pride."

At Pytor's shout, Maverick scanned the wall, finding Yaro nearby, dressed the same as Zander. He looked like a large boulder clinging to an even larger boulder. In an obvious race, he was gaining on Zander.

Zander glanced over his shoulder. His muscles bunched. That was all the warning Maverick got before he pushed from the wall, leaping toward a row of hanging hooks that led to a second wall. A gasp escaped Maverick as Zander hung mid-air. His first instinct was to catch him, but Zander easily snagged two of the suspended metal hooks. Using only his abs, he swung his body weight forward, finding two more hooks until he was quickly closing the distance between the walls.

Maverick was transfixed. He knew now where Zander got his amazing body. The strength, agility, and flexibility it took to pull off each move Zander made had Maverick going hard. Zander turned him on in every way. To Maverick's surprise, as big as Yaro was, he was gaining on Zander. They struggled on the hooks, fighting to stay ahead of each other and to control the best hangers. Zander held his own against the mountain.

"If you hurt my man, I'll break your face," Pytor yelled, making Maverick wonder which man Pytor considered his.

They made it to the wall almost simultaneously. Each man leapt, catching hand and footholds. A growl rose in Maverick's throat when Yaro shamelessly stomped Zander's hand, causing him to lose his hold. While Zander scrambled not to fall, Yaro raced ahead to an upper platform with pegs on either side. Once there, Yaro grabbed two pegs and used them to stab the walls repeatedly from side to side, climbing higher.

Obviously recognizing defeat, Zander pushed from the wall, leaping to the ground. Laughter rained down on them as Yaro reached the top.

"You win," Zander called up to him, sounding proud despite losing.

"He cheats," Maverick said, sending Zander spinning in his direction.

A bright smile pulled at his cheeks. Zander barely looked winded. "It's only fair. I cheated last time."

Maverick couldn't help but laugh at their antics. "So, this is how you stay in shape. This is an amazing setup. I'm impressed."

Yaro scrambled down the wall and leapt, landing in Pytor's waiting arms without even rocking him on his heels. Maverick found himself staring as their lips met. He was learning all sorts of new things today.

Zander spoke, tearing Maverick's prying eyes away from the couple. "We didn't have an expensive gym to go to growing up. All we had was the outdoors keeping us in shape. Cliff climbing and jumping off shit like we couldn't die." Zander shrugged. "Some things are harder to give up than others. We never grew out of this."

"So, you grew up with Pytor and Yaro?"

Zander's gaze skirted away. He headed toward a table where a bottle of water sat waiting for him. He cracked the lid. "In a manner of speaking." Zander polished off half the bottle. "Did we wake you?"

Zander's hair was pulled back tight away from his face, but a few strands had come loose in his climb. Maverick tucked them behind his ear. "Nah. Your house is huge. Nothing happening on this end is bothering anyone in the bedrooms." Their gazes met. Maverick's throat went dry. "The bed felt empty without you. That's what woke me up."

"You look so hungry right now." Zander shook his head and a gorgeous smile tugged at his lips. He set his water aside. "I must make you tired with my constant bullshit." Zander looked away as he made the claim.

A ridiculous thought hit Maverick. He wondered if Zander was used to being told he was worthless. Maverick couldn't imagine anyone saying anything like that to this amazing man, but sometimes Zander said things that bothered Maverick. He made Maverick think someone hadn't treated him as he deserved.

Without thought, Maverick closed the distance between them, uncaring of the sweat coating Zander's skin. His fingers found Zander's jaw, leaving Zander no other choice but to hold his stare. "What bullshit are you referring to? Your heated glances? I fucking love those." He took Zander's hand and led it to his hard cock. "I know you're not calling the sexy things you do and say bullshit. Everything about you keeps me hard. It's not possible for me to get tired of any of that."

Zander's fingers shaped Maverick's erection through his thin shorts. His expression punched Maverick in the chest. "Maverick, I—"

"Zander, you should get your man up on the wall. I'll race him."

Heat rushed to Maverick's cheeks at Pytor's bellowed words. Zander's body probably hid what they were doing from view, but still. "Goddamn. See what you do to me? I completely forgot they were here."

Zander's soft chuckle did nothing to help Maverick's erection abate. "He has to stay healthy," Zander called over his shoulder. "With sponsors coming to look him over, he can't risk getting hurt playing around with us."

"Let me practice a little first. Then, I'll accept your challenge another day," Maverick yelled, adding his thoughts.

Zander dropped his forehead to Maverick's chest. His shoulders shook with laughter. Maverick wrapped his arms around Zander and held on tight, rocking side to side. This man, he'd stolen Maverick's heart when he hadn't been looking. No one else made him lose his head the way Zander did.

Maverick's lips brushed Zander's ear. "I say we take a shower. In private. Where no one can see us."

Zander's body shook harder. When he spoke, each word laced heavily with laughter. "He said, get your man *up* on the wall. If he only knew."

A snort escaped Maverick. He couldn't help it. They were such a mess. Like teenage boys who couldn't control their hormones or keep their hands to themselves. "I blame you,"

Maverick said without an ounce of shame. "Hanging from hooks and jumping around all sexy. You're like a very fuckable spider monkey."

Zander's laughter turned into a guffaw. His guards both openly stared. Maverick steered him to the door while making monkey noises and holding Pytor and Yaro's gaze as he passed. By the time they reached the hallway, Maverick wondered if he'd be forced to carry Zander, his laughter had gotten so out of control. Even Maverick's heart smiled as he watched Zander trying to get himself under control. He was in love with this man. One day soon, he'd have to confront that. Today, he planned to fuck him in the shower.

CHAPTER 6

MAVERICK: *I'M MEETING GREEN at the bar to let him know I'm considering other offers. When I'm finished here, I'll come by and we can cuddle all night.*

It was the third time today he'd messaged Zander with no response. He tried not to worry since Zander had his finger in so many pies he never got to sit still. It was hard though. Maverick fought the urge to rush over there and check on him.

He had things to do first. He'd been putting Jude off for almost three months while he trained for his first circuit match. Maverick didn't have the heart to keep making excuses and dodging Jude's calls. It wasn't in Maverick's DNA to be dishonest. Before he could send another text to Zander, Maverick was interrupted.

"Since you wanted to meet here, I'm assuming you've decided against a contract with me."

Maverick motioned for Jude to sit. "That's not entirely true. Would you like a drink?"

"I wouldn't say no to a beer," Jude said, claiming the bar stool next to Maverick.

Maverick motioned for the bartender to bring Jude a beer. With new drinks in hand, Maverick focused on Jude. "When you first approached me, I didn't have much time to think about your offer. Now that I've had some time to talk it over with my man, who is way smarter about business dealings than I'll ever be, I've decided to enter one circuit match sponsor-less."

Jude nodded. "That makes sense. You have to look out for yourself, but you do realize you can enter a contract with me, and have other sponsors too, as long as they're not competing products. Not to mention, unless your man has some connections I don't know about, sponsors don't usually show up to no-name matches."

Against his will, a smile snapped to Maverick's lips. "Zander seems to think he can get Left Hook Energy Drinks and Coastal Clean Eats there."

"Zander?" Jude's voice turned hard at the question. "Do you mean Zander Kapra?"

Maverick nodded, feeling somewhat guilty. Despite Zander's pep talks, which sounded reasonable at the time, Maverick still felt like he was cheating the system somehow. Jude was right. Sponsors didn't usually show up to no-name fights. If he wasn't dating Zander, neither of those companies would look for him.

A self-deprecating smile touched Jude's lips. "I should've seen this coming. I have no problem with you being represented by Left Hook too, but Coastal is a direct competitor. Kapra played me hard with you."

Maverick's brows pulled together. "What's that supposed to mean? I'm the one who decided to do what's best for me."

The disbelieving chuckle coming from Jude sounded entirely too patronizing to Maverick's ears. "Let me guess, all this is your idea, but Zander had it first. You do realize that Left Hook Energy drinks and Coastal Clean Eats are both owned by your boy, right?"

A snort escaped Maverick without his permission. "Zander wouldn't pull that shit on me. He knows how I feel about him throwing his money at me."

Jude appeared genuinely confused. "How do you think I found you?"

Each breath Maverick took came harder than the last. He had a terrible feeling in his gut. "What? Are you saying that's all Zander too?"

Jude nodded. "Zander gave me a call and said there was a bet fighter I needed to check out. I should've known it was a game. He got me out there. I offered. Then, once he had you hooked on the idea of having a sponsor, he steered you toward choosing one of his companies instead. Honestly, I can't believe I was so blind. Zander wouldn't willingly hand me such an amazing fighter."

"But that doesn't make any sense," Maverick argued, even though it did. It made perfect sense. Maverick would never accept Zander's money. Zander knew it, so he found another way to buy Maverick. And Maverick had confronted him on it when Hendrix had alluded to the same damn thing. Zander had so easily made him believe it wasn't true—that Zander had captured Green's eye all on his own. Fuck. Maverick barely fought the urge to massage the spot in his chest where Jude had ripped out his heart by pointing out the truth.

Jude just kept talking—like Maverick wasn't silently dying. "I get that I can't offer you the kind of money Kapra can, but at least what I'm offering is honest money. Your boy can't say that. Keep that in mind."

Maverick's face screwed up in confusion against his will. "What's that supposed to mean?" He didn't like anyone insulting Zander, even if Zander had lied to him. Zander was his. No one talked shit about him.

A deep line appeared between Jude's eyebrows. He eyed Maverick and sighed before shaking his head. "I think you need to have a real discussion with your man before you get hurt, and I don't mean emotionally."

"You're the second person to get all cryptic with me about Zander. If you have something to say, just say it."

Jude shrugged. "Fine. If you want mafia money backing you, ensuring they'll tell you when to win and when to take a dive, then go for it. I'm trying to offer you a real sponsorship into the big leagues."

Maverick's mind blanked. Of course, he'd heard rumors about who really ran the league, but he didn't believe them. "I know a shit ton of fighters and not once have I heard of anymore intentionally taking a dive."

Jude's smile screamed that he thought Maverick was an idiot. "You wouldn't hear it, would you? Those contracts come with non–disclosures." Jude stood and pushed away from the bar. "Look, I'm not going anywhere. If you want to talk things over with Kapra, get some answers, and then get back to me, I'm cool with that. You've got my number. Thanks for the drink." Jude paused as if hesitant to say more before ob–

viously deciding he would. "You seem like an amazing guy to me, Maverick. I'd love to back you on your way to the top, but not so much I'd lie to you about anything. Even if you decide you don't want to work with me, I'll be around if you need me. Kapra is dangerous. I don't know how he'll react if he figures out he doesn't own you. If you need help getting out, call me."

Maverick wanted to lash out at the assumptions Jude kept throwing around, but too many things were clicking into place inside his mind. The security, everyone tiptoeing around him, and Zander never telling him much about his past. The accent that peeked out sometimes. Rather than snapping on Jude, since it wasn't his fault Maverick had been blind, he gave Jude a sharp nod.

"Thanks, man. I'll keep your offer in mind." After shaking Jude's hand one final time, Maverick motioned for the bartender to bring him the check. Even though he was certain Zander would never get mixed up with the mafia, it was time for them to talk. Maverick shook his head as he moved for the door. Even to him the idea seemed beyond ludicrous. No doubt, Zander would laugh his ass off over this one.

Pytor barely spared Maverick a glance as he came through the door. "He's in his office."

Maverick nodded and kept walking. He couldn't stop. If he did, he might lose his nerve. The moment he set eyes on Zander, he knew. Zander probably wouldn't be laughing at anything. In truth, Maverick wasn't sure Zander was capable of laughter as high as he was. White smoke filled Zander's office. It was so thick he could barely see. Maverick waved it away. His head spun from only walking through the haze. Zander looked a mess. His pink dress shirt was halfway unbuttoned, and his sleeves were rolled up to his elbows. Zander's hair stood in every direction.

"I've been texting you all day. What the fuck are you smoking?"

Zander shrugged. "Whatever Yaro dug up for me. I've had a rough day," Zander explained before sprawling out on his couch and covering his eyes. "To be fair, my birthday always sucks."

"It's your birthday?" Maverick couldn't choose a topic to be pissed about the most.

Zander peeked out from beneath his arm. "Don't sound like that. I don't celebrate the cursed day."

"This isn't celebrating?" Maverick didn't know why he couldn't stop with the accusations. He was just so goddamn angry.

"This is forgetting," Zander answered. His words came out slurred.

Maverick sat on the coffee table, braced his elbows on his knees, and leaned over Zander. He wished Zander would tell him why he was the way he was, or at least look at him.

"I need to ask you something."

A tiny smile touched Zander's lips, but he didn't uncover his eyes. "You're always welcome to ask me anything."

"Jude says if I sign with anyone you've set me up with I'll be forced to take a dive if ordered to do so."

An irritated sounding sigh escaped Zander. "How tiresome. No one has done that since the Conti."

Maverick blinked, trying to make sense of Zander's words. "What's the Conti?"

"Italian mafia." Zander's words slurred but Maverick heard him right. "They used to run the west coast until Gio Conti pissed off a contract killer for the Russian mafia. He wiped them all out." Zander swiped his free hand through the air as if Maverick didn't understand what wiping them out meant.

A pain bloomed in Maverick's head. He didn't know if it was from Zander's claim or the secondhand smoke. "Are you being serious?"

At Maverick's question, Zander sat up and took another long drag from a lit red cigar in the ashtray before focusing on Maverick. "Completely. The Conti's might have been Italian, but Gio, the family head, he was a huge fan of Russian street fighting. The brutality of it all appealed to his mean streak." Zander massaged his face, as if having trouble staying lucid. "Anyhow, he brought fighters here from Russia and started an underground league. He did a lot of leaning things in certain people's favor or a certain fighter's way, depending on how deep the bets were or if he was trying to gain someone's favor. Um." Zander rubbed his eyes and sucked in another long hit. "Gio thought, since he'd started the underground, he controlled everything. The power went to his head. Then, he tried forcing the wrong fighter to do things his way. Turns out that fighter, Jozsua I think his name was, he was married to a contract killer." A snort escaped Zander. "Didn't end well for Gio."

Maverick's mouth opened and immediately snapped closed. It all sounded … insane. Another thought occurred

CHARITY PARKERSON

to him. Zander, Yaro, and Pytor were all Russian. And Zander had once said something about being a street fighter. "Wait. Were you one of the fighters Gio brought over from Russia?"

Zander finished his cigar and sprawled out again before answering. "In a manner of speaking." Maverick wanted to growl at how cryptic Zander always was when asked about his past. He fucking hated it, but Zander kept talking. "Gio, he always found his way to the streets where I fought." Zander's accent thickened to a level Maverick had never heard as his words slurred even more. "He had crazy in his eyes. That's what I remember noticing first. Mama called him a *d'yavol*, a demon. She had no idea how right she was. If you won a fight, your family ate that week. That's all that was in my mind as he watched me with those demented eyes."

Maverick rubbed his chest. He hated the way Zander's words made him feel—like something horrible was coming, and Maverick would never unlearn what he heard here tonight. "What happened if you lost?"

"You died." Zander said the words so matter-of-fact.

Maverick couldn't draw a full breath. "Was it better for you, when Gio brought you here to fight?"

"He didn't bring me here to fight. I was brought here to warm his bed. My family was spared for my sacrifice." With his eyes covered, Zander waved his free arm wildly. "It's okay, though. He got all the Conti wiped out with his stupidity, and I got all this. So, you don't have to worry," Zander said, sounding half asleep. "No one will ask you to lose."

Maverick swallowed past his swollen throat. "Are you saying you're now the mafia boss around here?"

"I'm no boss."

"Hey, boss. I brought you another blunt."

At Yaro's appearance, Zander uncovered his eyes and focused on Maverick. "That was a complete coincidence."

Yaro glanced between them. "I'll come back."

Maverick couldn't look away from Zander. Everything hurt. He didn't know this man at all. "When you say you're the one who owns everything now, does that include Left Hook Energy Drinks and Coastal Clean Eats?"

Zander blinked as if he sensed a trap but was too high to avoid it. "Of course."

As the blow landed, Maverick's eyes fell closed. "Damn. I really wanted to believe you wouldn't do that to me." Maverick shook his head, trying his ass off not to' lose his shit. Even to his ears, Maverick sounded entirely too calm. "I honest to God thought you were only trying to help me not get screwed by sponsors. The whole time, you were setting me up to buy me, even though you knew I didn't want that. You really did a great job of making me think I'd earned those sponsors. I knew you were too good to be real, but I kept drinking in all your lies because I wanted everything you said to be true."

"Huh," Zander grunted, sounding resigned. "It's officially my birthday now. The curse continues."

The pain in Maverick's chest doubled. "You're not even sorry, are you?"

"For wanting all the best things for you? No."

Maverick pushed to his feet. "I was on my knees when I confessed some of my deepest worries to you. You stared down into my eyes and lied to me. I've never let myself be weak and real with anyone like I have with you these past three months. Thank you for reminding me why." With one final look at the person who'd stolen his heart and crushed it, Maverick headed for the door. It took every ounce of his strength to stop himself from looking back. His whole world was behind him, and it was all a lie.

"You're braver than me," Zander said, stopping Maverick in his tracks.

Maverick turned. He couldn't stop the hope rising in his chest. Surely Zander had something, anything he could say that would wipe away the past two hours of Maverick's life. He needed Zander to have the words to save them because he didn't.

Zander looked more lucid than he had since Maverick walked through the door. "The sheer depth of your courage never ceases to amaze me," Zander added once he had Maverick's attention. "Since day one, you've treated me like you can't be hurt. I'm not that strong. If life has taught me anything it's that I absolutely can be broken. But I've given you all that I am. All that I have to give. It's funny to me how you've spent the last three months trying to convince me that my money means less than nothing to you, but now you're leaving me because I tried helping you with it. I have to wonder, are you really upset I tried to help you with something you care nothing about? Or, are you simply jumping on the first excuse to walk away because you've been searching for a way out? Since I'm fucked up, and think I deserve no one, I'll always believe it was that second one. Either way, on your way out, please tell Yaro I could really use that blunt he found." On that note, Zander stretched out again, covering his eyes, and obviously done with Maverick. Maverick wanted to scream and fight, but his lungs no longer worked. Without his heart, everything else failed him.

CHAPTER 7

THREE MONTHS LATER. PRESENT day...

Punching and kicking a helpless bag was the only thing keeping Maverick sane. There was nowhere to go with his anger except Powerhouse Training where he worked out each day. He couldn't talk to anyone. Other than Zander, Maverick didn't have anyone. Zeke stood feet away, abusing another bag. Even though they'd been friends for years, Maverick couldn't make his tongue work. He couldn't tell anyone he'd fallen for a liar. That he'd lost his job. Nothing was right anymore. Each time he opened his mouth to speak, say anything at all, the words jumbled in his throat, and choked him.

"This kid will cure cancer one day."

At Zeke's yelled announcement, Maverick snapped to attention. His gaze swung the kid in question's way. Korey lived with Zeke. His older brother, Charlie had been Zeke's best friend before he'd gotten killed in Afghanistan. Zeke had taken Korey in after the man's death. His intentions had been pure, Maverick was sure. Now, Korey always watched Zeke, when Zeke wasn't looking, in a way Maverick understood too well. How sad for them both?

Under Zeke's open praise, Korey blushed.

A shot of compassion ran through Maverick. This child would be crushed when Zeke didn't love him back. Maverick knew. He was already there with Zander. He found himself joking with Korey, trying to make it better. "You'll need that medical degree if you keep hanging out with this guy," Maverick said, bringing Korey's unique gray stare his way. He was beautiful—like a perfect porcelain doll. Zeke was an idiot. Maverick wasn't. He kept talking, hoping to make Korey smile. "An old man fighting past his prime needs a good doctor in his corner." Zeke dodged as Maverick pretended to jab him in the ribs.

Korey's blush disappeared. Defiance flashed in his eyes, making him twice as hot. "Really? Who do you have lined up?"

An unexpected laugh burbled in Maverick's throat. He liked Korey. He had spunk.

"Let me grab my stuff and we'll head home," Zeke said, recapturing Korey's attention. Korey nodded. His hungry gaze followed Zeke as he headed for the locker room. Maverick couldn't take it. He filled the seat next to Korey.

"Are you coming to Vegas with Zeke this weekend for his match?" Zeke was the light heavyweight champion and was defending his title. He assumed Korey would be there. Judging by the way Korey's eyes skirted away, Maverick assumed wrong.

"I'm not sure," Korey answered as he shoved books in his backpack. "We haven't talked about it."

Considering it was Thursday and Zeke was fighting on Saturday, Zeke obviously had no intention of taking Korey along. Rage owned Maverick in that moment. What was it about rich, older men? Did they think everyone was just sitting around, waiting for them to find the time to love them? Fuck. Korey was twenty-two. Maverick was twenty-four. They should ditch everyone else.

"You should go with me."

Korey froze in the middle of zipping his backpack. For a moment, he stared at his hands before finishing the job. When he spoke, he sounded unsure. "Um. How do you mean?"

Maverick's resolve doubled. Korey was gorgeous. He didn't deserve to go unnoticed. Without thought, Maverick's voice turned sultry. He scooted closer. "I thought I could pick you up.

We could see the town afterward and you could stay with me."

Korey's beautiful gaze slid Maverick's way, but he didn't speak.

His interest grew. He was making the right choice by leaving the dream of Zander behind. "Or we could skip seeing the town, and you could just stay with me."

"The hell you say," Zeke barked behind him.

Korey's gaze snapped to where Zeke stood. He looked guilty. An irritated sigh rose in Maverick's throat, but he didn't let it fall. Korey had no reason to feel like he'd done anything wrong. The boy had come to the gym every day, after his final college class, for two years now, watching Zeke. His hot stares had been ignored. Now, it was Maverick's turn to show him some attention.

Zeke didn't let up. "Korey isn't ruining his life by getting mixed up with any of the no-good fuckers in this building."

Maverick didn't take Zeke's words to heart. A smile tugged at his lips as he watched Korey come to his feet. Fuck, he really was sexy with his perfect hair and runner's body. "Damn, Zeke. Tell me how you really feel. You should let the boy come out and play for at least one weekend."

Korey switched his gaze between them as if he didn't know how to react.

Maverick kind of liked keeping him on his toes. Most likely, Korey had never had anyone control him the way Maverick would, but he could learn.

Zeke didn't back down. "Let's go Korey." The way he headed for the door spoke volumes about how he expected to be obeyed without question.

Maverick wasn't that easily intimidated. Instead, he handed Korey's his number. "Think about my offer. Here's my number. Let me know."

"Let's go, Korey," Zeke repeated without looking back.

Korey didn't move right away. Instead, he held Maverick's gaze. One corner of Maverick's mouth lifted in a smirk. Korey would call. Maverick saw it in his eyes. He was every bit as tired of being jerked around as Maverick. Maybe he'd forget Zander after all.

"What the fuck are you doing?" Hendrix asked, filling the chair Korey had abandoned the moment the boy was gone. "Everyone knows Korey belongs to Zeke."

Maverick shrugged. "Then he should stop stringing Korey along."

Hendrix's light green gaze moved over Maverick's face, seeing too much. "I thought you were dating Kapra."

He couldn't hold Hendrix's knowing stare. Maverick's gaze skirted away. "No. It seems you were right about him."

"I didn't want to be right." Hendrix sounded so sincere, Maverick found himself focusing on him once more. "You deserve better," Hendrix added, holding Maverick's stare.

It was on the tip of his tongue to ask who was better than someone will-ing to buy him. Zander had gotten in his head with his parting shot. Why had he cared so much that Zander tried to help? Maybe he was scared he had a price after all, and Zander might find it. So, he'd ran before he found himself part of a monetary exchange rather than a love affair.

"I'm not sure that's true," Maverick said without thought.

Hendrix's lips parted in surprise.

Maverick couldn't take everyone seeing his shattered heart. He tried lightening the mood. Without thought, he slapped Hendrix's thigh and squeezed his leg above the knee. "Don't worry over me. I always land on my feet like a lion."

Hendrix winced.

"Holy shit. I'm sorry." Maverick rushed to make it better as he realized what he'd done. Hendrix had once been the top contender for lightweight champion before an accident shattered his leg and ruined his career. He had worked as a corner man ever since, and Maverick had completely forgotten all about that shit before slapping Hendrix's bad leg. He rubbed Hendrix's thigh. "Jesus. I'm a fucking idiot. You should punch me. It would make me feel better."

Hendrix set his hand over Maverick's, stopping his frantic motions. His face was pale, but his smile was sweet. Fuck. He'd really never noticed how beautiful Hendrix was. Maverick didn't understand how he'd been surrounded by so many great guys and never noticed a single one. "Stop. Please?" Hendrix begged. "You forgot, and that's what I love about you," Hendrix said, rubbing Maverick's hand one more time before pushing it away. "You're the only one who forgets." With a final smile, Hendrix pushed from the chair, and walked away. His limp was worse than usual, doubling Maverick's guilt. It was like he couldn't stop fucking up everything he touched. Maybe he hadn't run from Zander to save himself. Maybe he'd been saving Zander from him.

Korey: *Does your offer still stand for Vegas this weekend?*

Maverick: *Absolutely. If you'd like, we can leave tonight.*

Korey: *Sounds good. Just let me run home and grab some stuff.*

Maverick: *Awesome. I'll send you my address.*

Korey: *I'll be there.*

Zander: *Not answering my calls is beneath you.*

Zander: *I'll be in Vegas this weekend. Come find me. Hear me out. Let me fix things.*

Maverick shot to his feet when the knock landed on his door. Anything was better than staring at Zander's texts, even if it was some neighbor kid trying to sell him candy. He was more than a little surprised to find Korey on the other side. He hadn't expected the guy for a couple more hours, at least. Maverick eyed Korey. A self-satisfied smile pulled at his lips. Korey was just the distraction he needed. He motioned Korey inside. "Come in."

Korey waved off the suggestion. "No. I can't stay. Sorry. I hate doing this on such short notice, but I just stopped by to tell you I can't go to Vegas with you this weekend." Korey couldn't meet Maverick's stare.

There was something wrong. Maverick's smile fell. Korey never acted like this. "That's okay. Are you all right? Would you like to come in?"

"No," Korey answered, taking him by surprise. "I have to find a new place to live before it gets too late."

All Maverick could do was blink. He'd known Zeke would be pissed over Korey choosing to go to Vegas with him, but fuck. "Damn. That doesn't sound good. Come in. You can stay with me until you're settled."

Korey managed a smile. It was sweet. He finally met Maverick's stare. "I couldn't, but thanks."

Maverick snagged Korey's arm before he could get away and dragged him inside. "I wasn't asking. No offense, but you look like hell. Zeke would kill me if I let you drive away this upset."

Korey tried going back out the door at the mention of Zeke's name. "Fuck Zeke. He doesn't care about me, and I don't need anyone telling him where I am."

"Nope," Maverick said, blocking his exit. "You're staying," Maverick said, sounding firm even to his ears. He really couldn't let Korey drive in this shape. He'd never get over the guilt if anything happened to him. "I didn't say a word about telling Zeke where you are. You're a grown man. He doesn't need to know where you are at all times."

After eyeing Maverick for a moment, as if assessing his earnestness, Korey nodded. "Thanks. It's been a rough day. If you're cool with me crashing on your couch, I'd be forever grateful and out of your hair in the morning."

Maverick motioned toward the couch. "I have a guest bedroom and you're not in my hair. Things haven't exactly been great for me either today. You're doing me a favor by agreeing to keep me company."

Korey sat without argument. "Why was your day bad?"

Maverick chose the opposite end of the couch and kicked his feet up onto the coffee table. For a moment, he stared into space, trying to decide how much he should admit. Everything hurt. He didn't know where to start. Maverick shook his head. "It's nothing." He flashed Korey a smile. "Tell me about Zeke. I know he didn't put you out, so why are you looking for a place to live?"

Korey dropped his head back on the couch and eyed the ceiling. He crossed his arms over his chest as if the move could protect his heart. "I put myself out," he said finally. "Zeke never would've done it and it needed to be done."

Maverick bit back a sigh. Wasn't this a room full of fools? "How long have you been in love with him?"

Korey visibly blinked back tears at the question. That was a feeling Maverick understood too well. "Since day one. God," Korey breathed. "I'm such a dumbass."

Rage burned inside Maverick's chest on Korey's behalf. "No. He is."

At Maverick's outburst, Korey met his gaze, as if needed someone to be on his side.

Maverick didn't let him down. "A man like Zeke doesn't keep someone around and give them as much as he's given you unless he wants something in return. The way he watches you, I'd say he wants everything from you."

Korey snorted and went back to staring at the ceiling. "He's already had all of me," Korey said, taking him by surprise. The way they watched each other reminded Maverick of Zander and him before they'd hooked up that first time. "Now he's over it," Korey added, pulling Maverick's attention back on topic. A low curse escaped Korey, sounding like came from his soul. "Fuck. If you already knew about Zeke and me why did you ask me to go to Vegas with you?"

Maverick eyed him, going as far as to tilt his head to one side, wondering if he was overstepping. "I think we're a lot alike, and maybe we'd be better together."

Korey's eyebrows hit his hairline at the claim. "Better than what?"

A sad smile pulled at Maverick's lips. "Better than with someone who's never been told no. Someone whose money has bought them whatever and whoever they want. Just better," Maverick said, getting worked up. He looked away and crossed his arms over his chest, mimicking Korey's heart-shielding pose. "Yesterday... I don't know. I saw something in you." He shook his head and flashed Korey a sad smile. "Never mind. You're hot. We're young. Why don't we go ahead and hit Vegas? You can leave before Zeke's fight and get your things out while he's otherwise occupied. I'd make it worth your while."

Korey's lips turned up in the corners. "I'm tempted to take you up on that just so I'll stop feeling like I've been kicked in the balls."

"Let's do it then," Maverick said, shifting to his feet.

"But," Korey said, stopping him. "That wouldn't be fair to you."

Maverick's usual cocky attitude returned. He felt more like himself in that moment than he had since Zander wrecked him. "Babe, I'm eyes wide open and willing." His smile slipped. "You'd be helping me too."

Korey released a loud sigh, sounding exactly like a man who would regret him one day. "All right. Let's go," Korey said, coming to his feet.

Maverick fought the urge to jump up and down like a little kid. He didn't need Zander and his lies. Life hadn't come to an end the moment he'd walked away from Zander, ripping out his heart in the process. If he worked hard, he might survive the loss.

With Zeke's title match happening in Vegas, Zander knew Maverick would come. What surprised him was the number of familiar faces he kept seeing around his hotel—like everyone had chosen to stay at the Luna rather than the hotel hosting the fight. He'd also been surprised to learn Maverick had checked in. Zander had been prepared to stalk him anywhere. Once Zander heard he'd reserved a room with another man, everything became clear. Of course, he'd chosen this place. He couldn't punish Zander properly by being with someone else if Zander didn't see it. Maverick knew him well. He'd known Zander would follow him here.

Zander left Yaro to follow Maverick. His heart couldn't take watching Maverick treat a guy his age like precious glass. It didn't matter he'd done this to himself by coming here. The elevator door opened to take him to the top floor where he could get away from the sight of Maverick for a few minutes. Another familiar face filed onto the lift with Pytor and him. Hendrix didn't look Zander's way as the door closed them in together. Zander didn't know if the man purposely ignored him or was simply lost in his thoughts. The way his eyebrows pulled together in a scowl could've meant either.

They passed the third floor. Hendrix's hand shot out, hitting the emergency stop button, sending alarms blaring. Before Zander's shock cleared, a gun appeared less than a foot away, pointed at his chest.

Hendrix's light green eyes didn't scream insanity. They were clear. Hendrix had a purpose. Zander felt... resigned and strangely relieved. Peace had finally come for him.

"What the fuck is this?" Pytor roared, as he attempted to shove Zander behind him.

Hendrix's stare never wavered from Zander. His hand didn't shake. "I won't let you hurt Maverick. He doesn't deserve someone destroying his life and career so the rich can get richer. This has to stop. It should've stopped with Gio. Yet, you're running his businesses like he's still here."

He waved for Pytor to stay back. "Gio is dead," Zander said, because he got the impression Hendrix needed the reminder. Sometimes, Zander also needed the words said aloud, reminding him a monster was gone. "Everything terrible he stood for, died with him. You don't have to worry Maverick will end up like us. But I won't apologize for taking control of Gio's assets after he died. I took what was mine after almost twenty years of serving as his whore," Zander said, feeling the rage of a cruel life boiling inside him. He took a step closer to the gun. "I took what he owed me for the months I spent in bed, recovering from internal injuries and broken bones. He owed me everything for every bruise I hid. Concussion I suffered. I know he stole everything from you too. Let me give it back."

"I don't want your fucking money," Hendrix spat, sounding enraged. "I want you gone. You know how I ended up like this. You know it wasn't an accident. People like you and me, we're not worth the air filling this elevator. But people like Maverick, he still stands a chance. He's good. I think it's time we get off this rock and leave it to people like him. He loves you and you don't deserve it."

"You're right. I don't," Zander said, shifting even closer. "So, don't miss." He moved forward until the barrel touched his chest. "I don't want live to see another family move in and take over. My sanity can't withstand watching Pytor and Yaro forced to work for someone new, being whipped like animals for protecting a child." He gripped the barrel, moving it slightly to the left, over his heart. "Don't miss. I'm tired." His eyes burned. Zander didn't care. Losing Maverick was a final blow in a long and exhausting life.

Hendrix's body sagged, as if the life drained from him. Pytor snatched the gun and tucked it away. The elevator started moving again. Hendrix and Zander never broke eye contact.

"You love him."

Even though it hadn't been a question, Zander answered. "Yes."

"He loves you too."

Zander's sucked in a ragged breath. "I don't know why."

Hendrix looked away. "Maybe Gio didn't completely break you."

"Yes, he did."

Hendrix's unnaturally light green gaze swung Zander's way. "Maybe he did, but I think Maverick has been healing you."

The elevator stopped again. Zander turned away. The door slid open. "He doesn't want the job," Zander admitted, as he stepped off the lift. "And I don't blame him. It's too much to ask of anyone."

Pytor made sure the door didn't close. Zander met Hendrix's gaze one last time. "I was serious earlier. If you decide you need anything, come to me. I know you don't want anything to do with Gio's money, but I have no qualms spending it. You didn't deserve what he did to you."

A flash of pain crossed over Hendrix's features. He visibly swallowed. "Neither did you."

"Maybe," Zander said, walking away. He still hadn't decided if he was relieved or disappointed Hendrix hadn't killed him.

Going early to Vegas with Korey had been the worst and best thing for Maverick's soul. They'd had a great time, drinking, talking, gambling, and making late-night drunken confessions. He'd been surprised to learn the depth of Korey and Zeke's relationship. Zeke was a fool for pushing Korey away, but Maverick had a feeling it wouldn't last long. He'd played witness to the way they stared at each other too many times to believe otherwise.

At the other end of the spectrum, losing Zander was a constant gnawing ache that wouldn't abate no matter how much alcohol Maverick consumed. It was also damn hard to pretend he didn't see Zander sitting nearby. His gaze wouldn't stop sweeping Zander's way. Zander looked two steps beyond fucking sexy in his expensive business suit. He stared back at Maverick, openly daring him to look away.

"Who is that?" Korey asked over the top of the drink menu.

Maverick didn't have to ask him to clarify. Korey wasn't an idiot. "That's my version of Zeke," Maverick answered tearing his gaze away from Zander for the hundredth time. Even he heard the pain lacing each syllable.

Korey's light-gray stare moved in Zander's direction. He eyed the person who'd broken Maverick in every way. "Wow. He's really beautiful, Maverick. What the fuck made you ask me to come here with you after being with him? He's... whoa."

Irritation had Maverick swiping the menu from Korey's hands, forcing Korey to meet his stare. "Don't do that. You're right. He's beautiful, but

most liars are. Don't compare yourself to him. If you weren't in love with
Zeke, and wanted to give me a real
shot, he couldn't compete with you."

The bright smile that overtook Korey's face screamed that he thought
Maverick was full of shit. Maybe he
was. Maverick no longer knew himself. "It wouldn't matter if I wasn't
in love with Zeke. You'd still be in
love with that guy—liar or not," Korey said, showing how well he understood. "It's okay," Korey added, setting his hand on top of Maverick's. A
hint of pain crossed Korey's features.
"If he didn't scream at you that you
should go live with someone else and

let them support you, then you're already doing better than I am."

Ouch. Korey hadn't deserved that one, especially coming from Zeke—the person who'd intentionally put Korey in that position, making Korey dependent upon him. "You should come live with me," Maverick offered without thought. Once it was out there, Maverick didn't take it back. "I have a spare bedroom. Obviously, I can't keep you in the style you're used to, but you wouldn't be homeless."

Korey pulled away and sat back, shaking his head. "Don't worry over me. I've been thinking, maybe I should give up Stanford and head back to Alabama. Maybe moving to California in the first place was a mistake."

Maverick couldn't believe what he was hearing. Zander's presence was forgotten. "You have a full ride. Are you insane? Do you really intend to let Zeke steal everything from you, including your education and future?"

With a shrug, Korey shifted uncomfortably in his seat. "There's more to it than tuition. Once Zeke cleans out my savings account, taking the money I owe him for supporting me the past two years, I won't be able to afford to keep living in California, even if I don't have to pay for college."

He couldn't believe what he was hearing. Zeke intended to clean out Korey's savings? At least Maverick didn't have to worry over that.

"Wow. This is a small world."

Maverick's head snapped up as the words fell over the table. He looked up into a familiar set of eyes. A smile automatically pulled at his lips at the sight of Jude. "Hey. Maybe not so small since we're all here to watch Zeke's match tomorrow."

"That's true," Jude said, sounding congenial. His gaze slid Korey's way before coming back to rest on Maverick. "I know this probably isn't the time, but have you thought anymore about my offer?"

An invisible weight punched Maverick in the chest. He'd lost Zander. The emptiness was staring him in the face again with that one question. For a moment, he stared at Korey. His gray gaze moved between them while he kept a polite smile in place. Maverick couldn't fix himself, but he could help Korey. "Yeah, I think I'll sign that contract." He could give Korey a place to live with the money Jude offered.

Jude slapped him across the back, nearly knocking him from his chair. "That's awesome. Who's your friend?"

Korey's smile brightened. "I'm Korey."

With Maverick's agreement to work for him out of the way, Maverick was obviously forgotten. Jude reached past him and held his hand out for Korey to shake. "I'm Jude. Since I see Maverick's man over there, giving you both the death stare, I'm assuming you two aren't together. As a couple," he added, clearing up any doubts about this question.

"Right," Korey said, keeping his polite smile in place. "We're just friends."

"In that case, I have no interest in being just friends. Would you like to get a drink?"

Maverick dropped his gaze to the table to hide his smile. Jude didn't mess around when he saw something he liked.

A nervous sounding chuckle came from Korey's side of the table. "Um. Sure. I guess."

"Perfect," Jude said, moving to Korey's side and helping him to his feet. Jude's gaze moved Maverick's way. "We'll set up an appointment next week to get that contract signed."

Maverick dipped his chin. "Sounds good. Take good care of Korey. I'm keeping a close eye on him."

Jude's expression shifted, turning serious. "I am taking care of Korey.

Otherwise, you're likely to get him hurt," he added under his breath as he led Korey toward the bar. Maverick's stomach cramped at the accusation. His gaze moved Zander's way. Was Zander capable of hurting Korey if he thought Korey was a threat? Maverick would like to think Zander would never do such a thing, but then again, Maverick wasn't sure he knew Zander at all.

A beer landed on the table in front of Maverick a half second before Hendrix filled the chair beside him. At the sight of Hendrix's familiar light green gaze, a genuine smile pulled at Maverick's lips. For some reason, with Zander sitting across the room,

Maverick needed all the friendly faces he could get.

"Hey. Damn, everyone is here tonight."

Hendrix shrugged at Maverick's observation. "The hotel where the fight is being held is booked solid. Since a few of the other guys from Powerhouse were staying here, and the prices were good, I figured I'd come too." His gaze slid toward the bar. "I see you came with Korey after all."

"Only as friends," Maverick said before Hendrix could get the wrong idea.

"I doubt Zeke will see it that way."

Maverick shrugged. Considering everything he'd heard from Korey, Maverick wasn't sure he gave a fuck what Zeke thought. "Korey's headed home in the morning. He's not staying for the match."

To his surprise, Hendrix didn't ask why. Instead, he nodded toward the bar. "Who's that with Korey at the bar?"

"Is this for me?" Maverick asked, lifting the beer Hendrix had set in front of him. At Hendrix's nod, Maverick sucked back half the bottle before answering. "That's Jude Green."

Hendrix's eyebrows rose. "The guy who owns Green's Fighter Fuel?"

"Yep."

At Maverick's response, Hendrix eyed Jude a minute longer. "He's pretty damn hot for an old dude."

A snort escaped Maverick. He needed a laugh. "I'm glad we ran into each other. It's been forever since we had a drink."

"That's true. You've become boring."

Another chuckle escaped Maverick. He'd always liked Hendrix. Hendrix never held back a thought. "Some people might disagree."

Hendrix polished off his beer. "Some people or just one person?" Hendrix kept his gaze locked on where Korey and Jude stood as he asked the question, giving Maverick time to hide his wince. His gaze slid Zander's way. He was gone. Maverick fought the urge to leap from his chair and hunt Zander down.

"He left the moment I sat down."

Maverick's gaze shot to Hendrix at his claim. "Who?"

Hendrix pulled a face. "Don't do that. You know who."

Maverick's eyes skirted away. He hated that Zander still owned him when Zander refused to tell him a damn thing about himself, or the truth for that matter. Maverick rubbed the back of his neck. "Sorry. I'm..." He sighed and pasted on a fake smile, giving Hendrix his full attention. "What's going on in your life? How have you been?"

Hendrix's smile turned sweet, easing some of the pressure in Maverick's chest. "Would you like another drink?"

"Sure. Let me get this round."

Hendrix shifted to his feet. Before Maverick could guess at his intentions, Hendrix touched his lips to the corner of Maverick's mouth. Maverick froze. He didn't know how to react. If Hendrix had ever shown any interest in him, Maverick hadn't noticed. He noticed now. "I've got it," Hendrix said, walking away. Maverick's gaze followed him across the room. For the first time, he realized he wasn't the only one. Several heads turned as Hendrix passed. Hendrix walked with a slight limp, but it added to his appeal in Maverick's opinion. Otherwise, he'd be too pretty.

When Hendrix reached the bar, he stepped between Jude and Korey, making Maverick laugh. Hendrix had gumption. He stood up for what he thought was right. Hendrix obviously didn't think Jude hitting on Korey was right. Maverick shook his head. Life had been so damn eye opening lately. Maverick wondered if he knew anyone anymore, or if he'd always been blind. Hendrix glanced over his shoulder, meeting Maverick's stare. He winked. Hendrix was so fucking beautiful. Maverick felt nothing, except empty. He wanted Zander.

CHAPTER 8

WITH ZEKE'S FIGHT OVER and everyone celebrating, Zander was back at the Luna. Back to stalking Maverick. He was alone now. Zander couldn't look away. Judging by Maverick's inability to completely hold his head up, Maverick had passed shitfaced two hours ago and moved into a territory of unknown drunkenness. Zander had watched his every move all night. Last night too, which Zander should get a medal for since Maverick had brought another man with him to Zander's hotel. Of course, Zander hadn't killed the boy the way he wanted. It hadn't taken him long to put out feelers and learn the boy belonged to Zeke. Not to mention, if there was a chance in hell Maverick might take him back, Zander didn't want to lose it by hurting some child Maverick flaunted in his face.

Maverick swayed on his stool. Zander motioned for Yaro to intervene since he was closest. While Yaro and Pytor flanked Maverick, stopping him from falling out, Zander crossed the room. He winced as Maverick came into earshot.

Yaro was attempting to lure Maverick from the bar. "Mr. Kapra requests the pleasure of your company."

"Tell Zander he can go fuck himself."

Zander pressed against Maverick's back, boxing him in while Yaro and Pytor melted away. "Why would I do that when I can fuck you?"

Maverick's phone buzzed, keeping his attention from Zander. Despite being ignored, Zander refused to budge. He stood silently as Maverick brought his phone close to his face and drunkenly answered his texts.

Once he'd obviously done all he could to avoid Zander, Maverick's sexy honey-colored eyes landed on Zander.

"Did you say something about fucking me?"

Damn, Zander hated the way Maverick asked that—like Zander wouldn't be anything more than a one-night stand if he accepted.

"That depends," Zander said, sounding harder than usual even to his ears. "Did you bring that child with you to Vegas to taunt me?"

For a moment, Maverick blinked at him. Zander could practically hear him sifting through all his scathing thoughts to choose a retort. In the end, he turned away and said nothing.

Love made Zander stupid and mean. Then again, maybe he'd always been both those things. "I shouldn't have said that. It's not my business who you spend your time with." Zander ground his back teeth, fighting the urge to take it back. It damn well was his business. Maverick was his. "Tell me to fuck off."

Nothing.

Zander didn't give up. "Tell me you hate me, and I make you sick. Stand up and scream at me for doing what I had to do to survive when I had nothing else."

Still, Maverick wouldn't look his way.

"You don't want to talk to me." Zander pressed his forehead to Maverick's shoulder for a moment, hoping to stave off the pain. "That's fine. You can listen. A person doesn't need water to drown. I've been suffocating for so long I forgot what it felt like to breathe properly before I met you." Zander swallowed. He couldn't fix this. This was his life. There was no changing it. He needed Maverick to love him as is, including the ugly parts. "Don't take that away from me. Don't take away the only—" Zander dropped his forehead to Maverick's shoulder again. He squeezed Maverick's arms and held on. There was no sense in him continuing. Nothing he said would make Maverick accept something he couldn't. He kissed Maverick's shoulder one last time. "I'll leave Yaro with you. He'll make sure you don't die of alcohol poisoning and that you make it back to your room." He couldn't let go right away. His fingers wouldn't unclench. "I love you."

Zander pushed away before he ruined Maverick's life. He motioned for Yaro to watch Maverick as he headed for the lobby. He kept his head down as he made his way to the elevator. Zander didn't slow even when people called his name. He'd known Maverick was done with him before speaking with him or seeing him with another man. His heart just hadn't wanted to accept it.

At the lift, Pytor reached past him and pushed the up button to take them to the penthouse. Zander stared at his shoes.

"Is that really how you plan to announce you love me?"

Zander didn't allow hope to rise. Maverick's dry tone didn't inspire much confidence in him having changed his mind. He met Maverick's gaze. There was so much pain in Maverick's eyes, Zander wondered if his chest would cave. "I assumed you knew."

Maverick visibly swallowed. He glanced away. The elevator opened. "That makes sense," Maverick said almost too low to hear while still staring at something in the distance.

"I guess I thought you understood I love you too, and you didn't need to lie to me about anything."

Pytor held the door, keeping it from closing.

Zander motioned toward the elevator. "Come upstairs. We can talk."

Maverick still wouldn't look at him. He shook his head. "His name is Korey," Maverick said unexpectedly. "The guy who stayed with me last night," he explained as he started away, still talking and obviously done with Zander. "He's Zeke's man. I kept him company while Zeke did his pre-match shit. Unlike you, I have nothing to hide."

Zander stepped into his path. Alcohol made Maverick too slow to avoid Zander cupping his face and pressing his forehead to Maverick's. He held Maverick's stare. "Come upstairs with me."

Maverick shook his head. Zander could practically feel the hurt rolling off him. "I think I'll hop a flight home. This isn't my scene."

Zander didn't let him get away. "Come upstairs with me," Zander repeated. Desperation owned him. If Maverick walked away now, Zander would never see him again. He felt it in his gut.

Maverick leaned away, looking pained. "I—" Maverick's voice died. He rubbed his forehead. One small sway on his feet, and it was over. Zander caught him a half second before he hit the floor. With a sigh that could be heard over the crowd, Pytor closed the distance between them and slung Maverick over his shoulders in a fireman's hold.

"You couldn't choose someone lighter in weight and sturdier in alcohol consumption?" Pytor asked the moment they were alone inside the elevator.

Zander bit back a smile but held his silence. He swiped Maverick's hair away from his face. Even passed out, he was the sexiest man alive.

"He'll get over this," Pytor said, bringing Zander's gaze his way. Pytor's size and profession was a trick. His eyes always gave him away. Pytor was a gentle giant. He had a soft heart. "If he's worth having around, he'll understand."

Zander nodded. He hoped it was true. Zander loved Maverick, but he couldn't make Maverick comprehend a life he never would.

Each time he thought he had nothing left to throw up, Maverick dug deep for another round of dry heaves.

When he finally came up for air and looked around the opulent bathroom, the first thing his gaze found was a familiar looking red duffle.

Maverick didn't question how his overnight bag appeared in the bathroom of Zander's penthouse. He'd have been more surprised if it hadn't. With more than a little of his weight leaned on the counter, Maverick washed his face and brushed his teeth. He didn't think he'd been trying to kill himself with alcohol, but damned if it didn't feel like it now.

The walk back to the bed felt like it took five years on the bow of a ship in the middle of a hurricane. As he fell across the bed, he promised

God he'd never drink again. A pile of blankets fell across him. Maverick's eyes flew open. Zander leaned over him, tucking him in. He looked like he hadn't slept in weeks. Even though he had his hair pulled back at his nape, several strands had escaped the hair tie to frame his face. Black circles marred his pale face. Maverick's heart turned over in his chest. He didn't like worrying Zander.

"You should get some sleep."

A small smile touched Zander's lips. He didn't meet Maverick's gaze. "I will when you're past this. It would kill me if you'd died from alcohol poisoning. Would you like some water? You should drink something."

"I just drank all the water from the bathroom sink," Maverick admitted.

Zander's nose curled in an adorable way. "As long as you don't get dehydrated."

"Get some sleep," Maverick repeated.

Zander didn't back down. "I will when you're well."

Maverick hated Zander taking that stance over something Maverick had done to himself. He held up the covers. "Lie down with me. Sleep."

Finally, Zander's beautiful eyes slid his way. He eyed Maverick as if trying to gauge his seriousness. After a moment, he shifted positions and slid beneath the covers next to Maverick.

Even though he was still pissed off at Zander, Maverick tucked all Zander's stray hairs behind his ears and snuggled close. A sigh escaped him as his eyes fell closed. He just needed a few hours' sleep before he faced Zander's lies again.

Unfortunately, sleep didn't come. Instead, every unanswered question rose to the surface, choking him. "Make me understand," Maverick whispered before he could stop himself.

"I can't," Zander whispered back. "I'd never want you to know what it was like, being sixteen and catching the attention of a forty-six-year-old man with more money than God. To have your own family sell you. One day, I had nothing. The next, everything, except an ounce of happiness or any freedom. Once you've been bought and paid for, your happiness means nothing. Your wants—less than nothing. The best thing that ever happened to me before meeting you was his death." Zander sat up. Maverick's eyes shot open, scared Zander would leave. Instead, Zander stared into space, as if seeing something only he could. "I'm smart enough to recognize I cannot make you understand something you never will. No doubt, you had a normal life with first world problems. You don't know what it's like to have to literally kill to eat and go hungry more often than not. When I caught Gio Conti's eye, I was overwhelmed by a lifestyle I'd never imagined existed." Zander's gaze swung Maverick's way. His eyes were dead. Maverick wondered if he'd puke again. "If you can't imagine killing to eat, you can't fathom what I did for this life. Things I wouldn't want you to know. Things that seemed like nothing in comparison to what I'd come from." Zander's gaze softened. He tucked Maverick's hair behind his ear, making Maverick's heart turn over in his chest. "I get that—for some reason all your own—you want me to be ashamed. Contrite. I cannot. Not even for you. I need you to love me as I am, even the ugly parts, but I understand if you can't. Being normal isn't something I know how to do. Recognizing moral boundaries was lost to me a long time ago." Zander looked away and visibly swallowed. "Maybe we'll find each other in the next life, and you won't hate me there."

Maverick saw something in Zander a half second before Zander turned his head. Maverick was hurting Zander with his reaction to learning about his mafia ties. It was too early. He'd had too much to drink to know what to do. "I need a shower."

"Of course," Zander said, coming to his feet. "I'll leave you to it."

"You didn't want to join me?"

Zander's gaze snapped to his. The hope in Zander's eyes reinforced Maverick's decision. Zander was right. Maverick didn't understand what it was like to starve, be forced to kill, and have to use his body to survive. This man had been nothing but good to Maverick. It wasn't fair for Maverick to punish Zander for doing what he must. For all Maverick knew, he might've made the same choices. All Maverick knew right now was that he loved Zander. He wasn't ready to give up.

"If you'd like."

Maverick held Zander's stare and nodded. "As bad as I'm feeling, it might not be a great idea for me to go alone."

Zander's expression closed. Maverick could practically feel Zander's hope dying. He wanted to kick himself for not simply letting things go. Maverick scrambled to fix it.

"Plus, I'd really like to hold you for a little while."

Zander held out his hand to help Maverick stand. "You never have to ask for that."

Maverick wasn't sure how much he could live with, but he knew what he couldn't live without.

Zander silently followed Maverick, stripping alongside him. Maverick fired the shower to life. He pulled Zander inside with him as the water turned hot. Zander kept his arms wrapped around Maverick's waist and his forehead pressed to Maverick's nape as the water beat down on them from every direction. He didn't fool himself into thinking they were okay. His arms wouldn't unlock. He needed to cling to Maverick as long as Maverick would let him. Maverick might still be done with him. Zander couldn't beat hope into submission. With Maverick's nude body against his, Zander should be hard as a rock. Instead, he hurt. All over and to his core.

"I love you."

Zander sucked in a breath and squeezed his eyes shut at Maverick's confession. He couldn't draw a deep enough breath to satisfy the burning in his chest. He very much feared it was more than water running down his face.

"For real, I love you," Maverick repeated. "And, you're wrong, I would never, ever want you to feel ashamed. Not of who you are or anything you've done. But, fuck yeah, I'm pissed that I had to learn shit from other people. I'm doubly pissed you tried to fool me into taking sponsorships from your companies."

Zander's eyes burned. He couldn't understand why, but they wouldn't stop stinging. If Maverick wanted him to hate himself, Zander was there.

Maverick turned in his arms. He held Zander's jaw and forced Zander to hold his stare. "If you've got more bombs, hit me with them now. Don't you ever let me find out anything else from anyone other than you again. You're mine. This is love. I won't judge you unless you fucking lie to me again."

"It wasn't my intention to lie," Zander admitted. "I couldn't explain why the money means nothing. It's not easy to admit everything you have is because you were someone's whore." The words barely passed Zander's lips before he found his back pressed against the wall. A very angry Maverick hovered over him, looking thunderous.

"Don't you ever call yourself that again." Maverick's gaze dropped to where his fingers encircled Zander's jaw. He dragged his thumb down Zander's throat. His eyes follow the motion. Zander's hunger grew along with the heat in Maverick's stare. Maverick's lips parted on a breath.

"So beautiful," Maverick breathed. "Everything about you is so goddamn gorgeous." Maverick's gaze lifted. He met Zander's stare. Zander's mouth went dry at the heat in his eyes. "I don't know how to make you see what I see. It pisses me off that you planned to let me walk away without a fight because you don't believe you deserve love. That you tried to buy me because you didn't think I'd stay otherwise."

Zander wanted to deny it. He couldn't. Maverick had looked into his soul and seen him like no one else ever had. Zander didn't know how to fight for someone he wasn't good enough to have. No one could know every tainted detail of his life and still love him.

Maverick lifted his gaze and met Zander's stare. "To me, you're perfect." Maverick meant it. The truth was in his eyes. Zander couldn't look away. "It's like you were created just for me. You should be angry with me. I left, on your birthday, even when I could see you were hurting. Get mad at me. Make me pay." Maverick's tone dripped sex. He dragged Zander's bottom lip down with his thumb before dipping his head and capturing it with his teeth. Maverick nipped, drawing a gasp from Zander. "Call me a bastard," Maverick urged as he crowded Zander's space and brushed light kisses across his lips. "Warn me that you'll make me regret it if I ever leave again." Maverick cupped Zander's dick and massaged. "Hurt me like I hurt you, Zander," Maverick whispered against Zander's mouth before he claimed Zander's tongue.

Maverick's erection tapped his. Zander's brain itched with dark desire. Maverick had left. Walked away. Zander had almost lost him forever, and it was hell. Being without Maverick was his worst nightmare come true. Desperation boiled in his gut and tore at his skin. He might not have ever seen him again. Held him. Kissed him. Made love. Zander almost missed his chance to be inside Maverick the way he promised he would be someday. He always let Maverick have control. Look what Maverick had done with his power. He'd left. On Zander's birthday. Without knowing, caring, or understanding the crippling pain Zander had been in that day. Maverick was right. He deserved to be punished.

Without warning, Zander's palm collided with Maverick ass with enough force that Zander's skin stung. Maverick's reaction was swift. He melted against Zander with a deep moan. Zander did it again. Maverick's dick jumped. The sounds coming from the his throat almost doubled Zander over in lust. Instead, he pushed

Maverick away and stepped around him before shoving him against the wall. He molded against Maverick's back and sank his teeth in Maverick's shoulder.

"Yes." Maverick sounded desperate. "Like that."

Zander's fingers dug into Maverick's hips, urging his ass back. Zander dropped to his knees and bit the cheek of Maverick's ass. He didn't release him. Instead, he sucked with enough force, there'd be a hickey and most likely teeth marks. Maverick pressed against his lips as if seeking more. Moans filled the large shower. Without warning or any prep, Zander shoved two fingers in Maverick's ass, pulling a cry from him. It wasn't enough. He needed Maverick's pain. He needed Maverick to hurt the way he had when Maverick walked away. Zander worked a third finger inside. Maverick was too tight for this rough play. Zander couldn't stop, and Maverick was riding his fingers like his next breath depended on it.

Zander flew to his feet. His fingers found Maverick's hair. He pulled and twisted, controlling him. With the slightest urging, he had Maverick's head pulled back, baring his throat for Zander's teeth. He bit and sucked the side of Maverick's neck the way he had his ass. When he was certain he'd marked him, Zander used his grip on Maverick's hair to steer him toward the short bench inside the shower. He shoved him forward, urging him to cling to the bench for support, as he dragged Maverick's hips back. They had no lube. It was the treatment Maverick deserved.

"Do it," Maverick begged. "Make me hurt." The way he tugged at his cock, openly seeking relief, spoke volumes on how horny Maverick was.

Zander was there with him. He craved the pain. He fingered Maverick's asshole, stretching it to make room for his cock. Water ran between their bodies from the rain shower. Zander blinked away the drops. He couldn't look away from the sight of his crown disappearing inside Maverick's asshole. A cry reverberated from the walls, driving Zander forward. He impaled Maverick, going root deep with enough force that he lifted Maverick's feet from the ground.

Maverick's motions quickened. He jacked his cock at lightning speed. His muscles tensed. Zander fucked him hard and fast.

"Goddamn. That's it, Zander. Fuck me. Make me hurt. Show me who's the boss. Make me pay. Fuck. Oh, God." Maverick's asshole clamped down on Zander's cock, tearing a cry from his lips. Zander froze. Maverick's orgasm hit. His ass began to spasm, massaging Zander's dick. Milking him. His eyes fell closed at the sensation. Pressure climbed his shaft. Zander dug his fingers into Maverick's hips with bruising force, holding him in place. A gasp tore from his throat as cum burst from his crown, filling Maverick's ass. Maverick gasped and moaned as Zander's hips ground against his ass, trying to get as deep as possible. He needed to imprint himself on Maverick's soul. When the last wave passed, Zander dragged his short fingernails down Maverick's sides, leaving claw marks behind as his cock slipped from Maverick's tight ass.

The moment he was free, Maverick spun. His mouth slammed against Zander's. Zander tasted blood. Maverick's tongue shoved its way inside. He sucked and stroked. Their bodies slipped against each other. Zander's feet left the floor. Maverick swept him up into his arms. His jaw flexed as his long stride ate up the floor, carrying Zander from the shower to the bed. The water still ran behind them.

Maverick glanced down. Their gazes collided. Passion burned bright in Maverick's eyes. His voice was hard when he spoke.

"I'm taking you to bed, Zander. Once there, I'm locking my jaw around your dick—hard or not. I'm sucking until you beg me to leave you alone. Once you're drained dry, I'm rolling you into your stomach, spreading those sexy cheeks, and fucking your asshole raw until you can't stand or sit without thinking of me." He set Zander on the mattress. His gaze never wavered. "This is forever. You and me," he said, stabbing a finger in Zander's chest before tapping his own. "So I suggest you figure out that you're worthy of this, because I'm not going away."

Zander couldn't tear his gaze away from Maverick's intensity. This man... goddamn. He left Zander speechless in the face of his untainted love. He saw Zander in a way no one did. Zander didn't know if he'd ever feel like he deserved Maverick, but he wanted him, and Zander never denied himself anything. He'd never let Maverick go.

With Zander still sleeping, Maverick tiptoed through the penthouse. He knew from experience, the hotel staff always stocked the kitchen before Zander's arrival. Maverick's sexy man was getting breakfast in bed. He'd earned it.

"I'm glad you came to your senses," Pytor said, startling Maverick. He was so used to the huge guard always hovering in the background without speaking, Maverick nearly jumped out of his skin to hear his voice behind him.

With a spoon still hanging from his mouth, two yogurt containers and two juice bottles in his hands, Maverick faced the giant guard. He sat kicked back at the kitchen table with his feet on the table and legs crossed at the ankles.

"What?" Maverick mumbled around the spoon.

Pytor dropped his feet from the table to the floor and held Maverick's gaze. "Zander needs you, so I'm glad you came to your senses. He's never had a nice man. You have to give him slack when he doesn't know how to handle kindness."

Maverick couldn't believe this man who was paid to keep a mafia boss safe was talking to him about this. After shifting his load, Maverick pulled the spoon from his mouth. "What do mean he's never had a nice man? A man left him millions." Then Zander had turned that into billions.

Pytor scoffed. "Not willingly. If you ask me, that man was no better than a pedophile—the way he scooped Zander from the streets when he was only sixteen. Gio never gave Zander anything but bruises, broken bones, and more issues than a mental patient. The man who killed Gio, he was a professional and a godsend. He made it look like Conti left everything to Zander because he believed—as we do—Zander is the only one standing between the West Coast and another family moving in. He wanted the West Coast and the fight clubs to be free of all that bullshit. No one questioned the legitimacy of the will. There were no Conti left to challenge it, and Zander had been running most of Gio's businesses for years."

Pytor could've told him anything, but—honestly—Maverick hadn't heard a word past bruises. He'd been sickened to learn Gio had bought Zander from his family when he was sixteen. To know the bastard had been abusive too, it was too much. Maverick wanted him double dead.

After shifting to his feet, Pytor moved around the kitchen, finding a wooden tray, and unloading the food in Maverick's arms. He kept talking as he arranged the food and added fruit to the haul.

"The Conti, he was sickeningly obsessed with Zander. He brought Yaro and me from Russia to watch him, ensuring no one looked the boy's way. He was possessive and sadistic. Gio was also convinced his enemies would try stealing Zander to use against him." Pytor shook his head. His eyes took on a sad tint. "I am ashamed to say, it was also our job to ensure the boy did not run." With Zander's breakfast tray looking like a professional chef had designed it, Pytor handed it to Maverick. "We've been very happy to see him smile."

Maverick accepted the tray, speechless. He'd learned more about Zander in one conversation with Pytor than he had in months of being with Zander. Now, all Maverick wanted to do was be everything for the man he loved—give him all the things he'd never had.

"I intend to make him smile a lot more," Maverick said, finding his words. He headed for the door intent on doing just that. Maverick almost made it to the hall before another question occurred to him. He turned back and focused on Pytor. "Why doesn't Zander celebrate his birthday?"

Pytor's eyes fell closed for a moment. When they reopened, they looked dead. "Shortly before Zander turned eighteen, he disappeared. It didn't take long for Gio to find a teenager with no money, living in the country illegally. As punishment, Gio brought Zander's little brother here for Zander's eighteenth birthday, let them visit for two hours, and then killed the boy in front of Zander. He said, for every time Zander tried to run, he'd watch another member of his family die a worse death than the last. Zander hasn't celebrated his birthday since."

With one final nod of thanks, Maverick carried the tray to the bedroom. He needed to set eyes on Zander, ensuring Zander's happiness. He felt sick over Pytor's revelations. Maverick couldn't get back to Zander fast enough. He needed to make Zander's life better. Most of all, he needed to prove he accepted every part of Zander—loved all of Zander, ugly past and all. The bed was empty as he came through the door. Before he had time to be disappointed, the bathroom door opened, and Zander stepped out. His hair had obviously been brushed, but he wore nothing more than a white t-shirt and underwear. Maverick had never felt so much pride as he did each and every time he set eyes on Zander.

"I was about to go searching for you."

A smile tugged at Maverick's lips at the confession, wiping away the ugliness of Pytor's story. He set the tray on the dresser. "In your underwear?"

Zander shrugged. "There's no one here who hasn't seen me in less." He crossed the room and stared down at the breakfast Maverick and Pytor had put together. "What's all this?"

Maverick couldn't stand another second of not holding Zander. He wrapped his arms around him from behind, molding his body against Zander's. "It was supposed to be breakfast in bed, but you woke up too soon."

A soft chuckle escaped Zander. "I could get back in bed."

Maverick brushed his lips across Zander's ear and caught a glimpse of their reflection in the mirror above the dresser. Zander looked amazing in Maverick's arms. He was smiling.

Maverick held tighter. "What can I do to keep you smiling today?"

"You're doing it," Zander answered without hesitating.

That wasn't enough. He needed to give Zander everything he'd never had. "What if I gave you another day of letting you have whatever you want—no regrets or complaining?"

The way Zander's face lit let Maverick know he'd made the right decision. "A full twenty-four hours?"

Maverick nodded. "Of course."

Showing his shrewd side, Zander didn't let up. "Starting now or when we get home?"

In that moment, Maverick would've agreed to anything. "How about we start now, but the no complaining clause doesn't end until it's been a full twenty-four hours back home?"

Zander's expression shifted. He bit his bottom lip, looking worried. "Can we start in a minute? I want to tell you what I want to do with my full day of spoiling you. Otherwise, I'll always wonder if you went along with me because you promised not to scoff."

"Okay," Maverick said, dragging out the word. He couldn't think of thing Zander would say that Maverick would scoff at, especially since he was all about making his man happy. "Hit me with it."

"I'm moving you in with me."

Maverick blinked. His mind blanked. Of all the things he might've expected Zander to say, that wasn't one. Before he could think of a single damn response, Zander kept talking.

"Before you tell me you don't need me to take care of you, I know you don't need me. This isn't about money or anybody owning anyone. I love you," Zander said, holding Maverick's stare in the mirror. "This is about me wanting to share a life with you. I want all your days and nights."

Without warning, Maverick's throat swelled, and his eyes burned. For the first time, he saw what he'd been fighting. Zander had never been trying to buy him. Maverick was the one with the issue. He'd been so busy trying to prove he was worth keeping, even though he couldn't match Zander financially, he'd ignored what Zander had been telling him all along. This was love. They were supposed to be working toward making a life together because they didn't want to be apart. He didn't need to prove to Zander he didn't want his money, because Zander didn't care about it at all.

Maverick swallowed past the lump in his throat. "You are the very best thing that's ever happened to me. I want your every day and night too."

Zander looked so hopeful it made Maverick's chest hurt. "So, I can keep you?"

"We're keeping each other." Maverick laughed. Happiness swelled inside him, taking control of him. "I can't believe I fell in love with a mafia boss."

A loud huff escaped Zander. "I told you. I'm not—"

Maverick tilted Zander's head back and captured his lips, cutting off Zander's argument.

Rapid knocking landed on the bedroom door. "Boss, do you want me to
call and get the plane ready?"

Laughter vibrated through their kiss.
Maverick no longer knew whose it
was.

"I swear that's just a coincidence."

"Give us two hours," Maverick called
out, sending Yaro on his way. He
spun Zander and set him on the edge
of the dresser.

Zander didn't release his hold
on Maverick's shoulders. His eyes
flashed with mischief. "What could
we possibly need two hours for?"

Maverick picked up the juice. "I
need to feed my man." He inten-

tionally poured juice down the front of Zander's shirt. Zander laughed while Maverick released an obnoxious gasp. "Oops. Now, I also have to clean my man."

Zander's laughter was the sexiest thing Maverick had ever witnessed. No one would ever steal it from him again. Not on Maverick's watch. He couldn't fix the past, but he would be the future.

CHAPTER 9

ONE YEAR LATER...

Back-to-back meetings were kicking Zander's ass. All he wanted was to be with Maverick. Of course, it seemed even Zander's showers weren't safe these days from his resentment for stealing his time away from Maverick. Every second they spent apart was murder. All Zander did anymore was rush to see his sexy fighter. Zander bit back a growl when his phone buzzed on the way to the car.

If one more person asked him for one more thing, Zander would fire them. Yaro held open the back door. Zander fished out his phone as he slid inside the car. Maverick's name brought a smile to his face.

Maverick: *Check your voice recorder app.*

Zander: *I have a voice recorder app?*

Maverick: **sigh* it looks like a microphone.*

Zander flipped through his screens. He spotted the tiny picture of a microphone. There was one recording available. "Huh. Who knew?" Zander hit play.

Maverick's voice filled the car. "I know you have a busy day filled with boring meetings. Just know I have a day filled with sweaty men, and not in a good way. Even though life pulled us in different directions today, I know I'll think of you all day. Miss you like crazy and love you even more."

"He is nice guy. You should keep him," Yaro said, voicing his opinion, which was unusual for him.

"I think I will." After a full minute, Zander realized he was smiling at his phone like an idiot. He was stupid in love with Maverick. Zander didn't know where to go with it sometimes. He wasn't sure Maverick was ready to hear exactly how much Zander wanted from him.

Zander: *That made my day. I miss you like crazy too, love you even more, and can't wait to see you.*

Maverick: *Check your left pocket.*

He didn't hesitate to dig through his left pocket. Zander pulled out a tiny heart-shaped chocolate and a note Maverick had obviously slipped in there at some point. He unfolded the note and read.

Eat my heart. Do it. You know you want my sugary goodness in your mouth. I promise I'll bring a smile to your face.

With a chuckle, Zander unwrapped the candy and popped it in his mouth before picking up his phone again. There was an unread message from Maverick.

Maverick: *Admit it. You ate it. You ate my heart, you sick bastard.*

A loud snort escaped Zander. He hugged the phone to his stomach and stared out the window. Still, his smile wouldn't abate. He had no idea how Maverick always managed to find the smallest ways to wow him, but he had completely swept Zander away, filling in every dark space with light. He couldn't wait to see what Maverick had planned next.

Taking Pytor's advice to heart, Maverick was easing Zander into celebrating his birthday again. As much as Maverick wanted to go all out, he understood Zander not wanting to have a party on the date of his brother's murder. On the other hand, Maverick craved fawning over the day his man was born. He hoped, since it had been twenty-one years since his brother's death, Zander would let him make new and happy memories for the day.

It had fully been his intention to go small. A nice dinner at an expensive restaurant. Wine, candlelight, and heated glances. Maybe the occasional sneaked feel beneath the table. Each time Zander looked his way with his bottom lip held between his teeth, a different craving rose inside Maverick. He wasn't sure he could go another day with this desire burning in his gut.

"I love you."

Zander said the words before Maverick could. Maverick didn't hesitate in returning them. "I love you too. And, I know you don't want to hear it, but happy birthday." At Zander's wince, Maverick scrambled to fix it. "Should

I start saying, thank god the love of my life was born today, instead?"

A small smile hovered on Zander's lips. "Baby, you can say whatever you like. It'll just take me time to adjust."

"You are the love of my life, you know?" Maverick said, turning serious. He needed Zander to understand how their lives were entwined now. With three sponsors backing him, including Green, Maverick didn't need Zander's money. Not that he ever had, but he couldn't live without his other half. "There's absolutely nothing I wouldn't do for you, but there's a hell of a lot I'd do to keep you."

Zander's gaze softened the same way it did when Maverick kissed him. The oxygen thinned in the room. Maverick found himself leaning closer. He didn't want to miss a word Zander had to say. Zander's expression shifted, turning nervous. He toyed with his napkin.

"There's something I've been meaning to talk to you..."

When Zander's words died, and he focused on something over Maverick's shoulder, Maverick followed his gaze. "Is that Jude?"

"Yes. The world is very small."

"Is he with—"

"It would seem so," Zander said, cutting him off.

"Holy shit. Are they—"

"Yep," Zander said, sounding every bit as shocked as Maverick felt.

"I can't look away. If I keep sitting here, I'm afraid I'll keep staring all night. Should we—"

"We should get the check."

"I'll get the check," Maverick said, motioning for their waiter. This new development definitely cramped Maverick's plans, but some things a person couldn't ignore or unsee. When their waiter appeared at the edge of the table, Maverick shoved enough bills his way to pay for their meal and a sizable tip. "Sorry. We have to go."

Maverick led Zander from the restaurant. They moved faster than necessary. When the night air hit them, Zander was the first to break. A loud laugh burst from him. Maverick couldn't look away from the sight of Zander's happiness.

"Did we just run from something supremely stupid?" Zander asked, holding his side and chuckling. The wind blew Zander's hair in his face. A huge smile stretched his lips. The moon and the ocean were the perfect backdrop for the perfect man.

Maverick's feet moved, closing the distance between Zander and him. His hand went to his pocket and his fingers encircled the gold and platinum ring he'd kept hidden all night. Before he could drop to one knee, Zander did. His chin hit his chest. Maverick could only blink at the sight of Zander at his feet.

"Maverick Abney, I know you're probably not ready. I'm equally certain you don't wish to be tied to some man fourteen years older than you. But there's no one else I'd rather spend a second with, much less my life. I'd love for this day to finally be remembered for something good. Will you marry me?" Before Maverick responded, Zander scrubbed his face and came to his feet. "Don't answer me. I'm an idiot. I don't have a ring or anything. There's nothing special about this moment."

"Everything is special about this moment because you're here," Maverick said, pulling the ring from his pocket. "I brought a ring."

Zander stared at the golden band Maverick held. His gaze moved from Maverick's hand to his face. "Are you being serious?"

A smile burst from Maverick. "You beat me to the punch. I planned to slip this in your pocket instead of candy this morning, but I lost my nerve.

I worried you'd see the ring and decide not to come home. Then, I worried, since it's your birthday, you'd feel like I wasn't respecting your brother's memory." Maverick knew he was babbling but he couldn't stop. "The thing is, no matter what the date says on the calendar, I don't want to spend another one without matching last names. Age doesn't matter, and I'm pretty sure I've been ready since three weeks before we met. I just want—" Zander's mouth covered his, cutting off Maverick's nonstop chatter.

Even as Zander's tongue stroked his, Zander pried the ring from Maverick's hand. With a final brush of lips on lips, Zander pulled away. Maverick watched as he slipped the ring on. Something shifted in his chest. He'd always known Zander was his, but seeing Zander wearing his ring doubled Maverick's possessiveness.

"Sometimes, I think Yaro can see the future."

Maverick blinked. Of all the things Zander could've said in their moment, that wasn't one Maverick would've picked. "What?"

Zander smiled, melting Maverick's heart. "Tonight, on the way home, he said I should keep you. Since I already have you, it seemed an odd thing to say. Now, his words make perfect sense."

"Well, I should admit, Pytor and Yaro helped me pick out the ring."

Zander looked down at his hand. The light hit the gold and platinum piece. It was unusual. Perfect for the unique man who wore it. "So, the boys have been plotting against me."

Maverick tilted Zander's chin up and pressed a soft kiss to the corner of his mouth. "What can I say? They love me. They think you should keep me. Have you decided yet if you will?"

"Fuck," Zander cursed, pulling a chuckle from Maverick. "I never answered. Yes, of course. Wait, I asked first. You should've been the one to answer."

"I gave you a ring," Maverick argued. "Jesus, can't you just marry me without arguing over it? I plan to marry you, even if you want some big, expensive wedding that's going to make me crazy. No doubt, you'll want me in a hundred-thousand-dollar suit or some shit, when Vegas literally has drive-thrus where you can get married, and you can charter a private plane that could have us there in a matter of hours."

Zander's whole body shook with laughter. "You could use a hundred-thousand-dollar suit."

"Are you serious?" Even Maverick heard the horror in his voice.

"Of course," Zander said, sounding pragmatic. "You never know when that might come in handy." He walked away, leaving Maverick floundering.

He chased after him. "No one needs that expensive of a suit. Do you know how many homeless people we could feed with that much money?"

Zander glanced over. "Do you?"

Maverick hadn't expected to be questioned. "Well, no, but I imagine it's a fuck ton."

"Okay," Zander said, linking fingers with Maverick and headed for the car.

"Okay, what?" An agreeable Zander was a reason to be suspicious.

"Okay, we'll give a hundred-thousand to a homeless shelter and we'll fly to Vegas tonight instead."

Maverick had the oddest feeling he'd just been maneuvered. "All right."

Zander stopped and met his gaze. "I love you."

"I love you too." Maddening or not, Maverick loved this man more than life.

"Life with me won't be boring."

Maverick knew that shit was right. There hadn't been a dull moment since they'd met. "Thank you." Maverick couldn't hold back the words.

"For what?" Zander asked, as he slid inside the car.

Maverick waited until Yaro shut them inside before tackling Zander in the seat and placing kisses every spot he could reach on Zander's face. He loved the sound of Zander's laughter. He couldn't wait to spend his life listening to it. With his forehead pressed to Zander's, Maverick stared into the light blue eyes that had captured him across the room nearly two years ago. "Thank you for not making me wait to have you as mine. I will never make you sorry." Maverick meant every word. For as long as they both lived, Zander would only know kindness and love.

Please keep an eye out for book three, *Sugar Bear.*

If you'd like to learn more about the demise of the Conti's, Jozsua's book is

.

ABOUT THE AUTHOR

CHARITY PARKERSON IS AN award-winning and multi-published author with several companies. Born with no filter from her brain to her mouth, she decided to take this odd quirk and insert it in her characters. One of her greatest loves is writing morally gray characters. You'll find them scattered throughout her hundreds of titles.

*Nine-time Readers' Favorite Award Winner

*2015 Passionate Plume Award Finalist

*2013 Reviewers' Choice Award Winner

*2012 ARRA Finalist for Favorite Paranormal Romance

*Five-time winner of The Mistress of the Darkpath

Connect with her online:

*Sign up for her newsletter: https://bit.ly/charityparkersonnewsletter

*Join her readers' group on Facebook: http://bit.ly/CharitysTribe

*Website: https://www.charityparkerson.com

*A list of her social media accounts and giveaways all in one place: http://hy.page/charityparkerson